OLD BONES AND NORTHERN MEMORIES

Written by Cully Gage
Cover Photo by Hoyt L. Avery

Copyright 1991
by Cully Gage
and
Avery Color Studios
Marquette, Michigan 49855

Library of Congress Card No. 91-76053
ISBN-0-932212-70-0

First Edition—September 1991
Reprinted—1992

Published by Avery Color Studios
Marquette, Michigan 49855

Printed in Michigan, U.S.A. by
Lake Superior Press
Marquette, Michigan 49855

TABLE OF CONTENTS

FOREWORD

Old buggers from the U.P. are hard to kill but The Reaper has been doing his best lately to make me extinct. Nevertheless he's failed so far and I'm determined to make it through the winter and be back at my lakes in arbutus time next spring.

Not content with hitting me in my old age with arteriosclerosis, ventricular tachycardia, phlebitis and diabetes he recently took a swipe at me resulting in congestive heart failure. It wasn't a particularly pleasant experience.

Awakening one morning I found myself desperately gasping for air, coughing hard and interminably, and with my heart going crazy with fibrillation, racing so fast I could not feel a pulse. There were moments when it not only skipped beats but stopped completely. I've had heart trouble before but nothing so utterly devastating. Waves of darkness swept over me but somehow I fought them off. I now recall that I had no fear of the death that I thought was happening. Nor was there any acceptance of it either. Instead I was angry, if anything. Nothing was going to keep me from seeing the forests and streams of my Shangrila. Nothing! After all, I'd had my first heart attack twenty four years before and had survived it. I would do it again. Somehow I did!

How long did it last? I have no idea. Time stopped whenever my heart did. I do remember once in the midst of my struggling that I looked at my bedside clock and it said five minutes past six, the exact time that Milove had died six years before. I knew because I have never reset that kitchen clock of hers. What is even more eerie is that my heart failure occured on the same date that she passed away.

When, a day later, I had recovered sufficiently to see my doctor he examined me carefully then told me I'd had a "textbook" case of congestive heart failure, that my old heart muscles had become too weak and tired to pump the blood back from my lungs, hence the gasping and dry coughing. He said I'd been very lucky but that, since another similar episode could occur at any time, I should put my affairs in order immediately. After giving me some prescriptions for various drugs he also gave me a big handful of don'ts. Don't ever get out of breath! Don't lift anything heavy! Don't get excited or angry! No, of course I couldn't go deer hunting nor drive my car. When I asked him facetiously if, at the age of 85, I should also abstain from sex he didn't smile but rebuked me. "You're in grave danger," he said. "Don't make light of it. Your days are numbered." If I behaved myself, rested a lot and took it very easy perhaps, just perhaps, I might see my lilacs bloom next year again if I were very lucky. He sure didn't seem very optimistic.

The Clock That Stopped

Well, so be it! It's not easy changing one's life style even when you know you must. I had to discover that I could plant only two tulips at a time, not three, that I had to rest three times going to the mailbox and four times on the way back, that I could not bring in an armful of firewood from the barn, and especially that I had to avoid all real effort and stress. My heart was my teacher. It told me in no uncertain terms whenever I had exceeded my limits, limits that kept shrinking from day to day.

But you do what you must do. Long ago I learned that lesson and to accept the dictates of fate without undue protest. Whatever adjustment it takes I'm returning to my homeland next spring and meanwhile I'll live each day as joyously as I can.

So, my friends, I'm writing another happy little book - this one about the last days of Cully Gage

3821 W. Milham
Portage, MI 49002

or
Hell
or
Heaven

8

DAY ONE

Most happy old men and women have discovered the secret for making the last years of their lives enjoyable despite the physical troubles and other miseries. That secret is this: It is possible to live two lives simultaneously. Children live only in the present; the young and middle aged live in the present and the future with all the anxieties these entail. Without much of a future yet freed from the need to work or raise a family, old people have the time to indulge themselves by recalling the good memories of the past as they go about their daily activities. Let me illustrate how I have done so in these, my dessert years.

This morning, awakening at seven, I sat on the edge of the bed for a few minutes to prevent the blackouts that occasionally occur upon arising due to my poor circulation. As I sat there, suddenly I was a boy again, leaping out from the bottom bunk of the Old Cabin, galloping nakedly down the hill path to our wilderness lake, then launching myself into the cold water. When my joyful splashings startled a nearby loon to skittering across its surface I echoed the wild laughter, shook my tingling hide dry, then ran up the hill again to make my breakfast.

That memory was so vivid it almost erased the realization that I was tottering rather than walking down the hall to the bathroom on legs that hurt. (They always do after being inactive.) While dressing I chanted "Old bones! Old bones! Damned old bones!" but I felt much better after sliding down the bannister railing of the seventeen steps as I and my children used to do when they were very small. How they'd squeal and beg for just one more ride. I could almost hear their young voices. Old men don't have to be dignified and I felt much better having done so.

As usual, before I made the coffee, I poked my head out of the back door to greet a new day. "Hello, world!" I whooped. So far that world has never answered me nor have my neighbors who live on the far side of my east soybean field. Yes, it would be another fine autumn day and to celebrate I gave the old farm bell a couple of strong tugs. I love the sound of that bell early in the morning.

As I filled the filter of my automatic coffeemaker and threw in the water, again I suddenly found myself a boy. This time I was fifteen on the mossy shore of Log Lake making a birchbark pail for our morning coffee. Arvo Mattila and I had hiked up there the night before hoping to catch some of the lunker brook trout that always swam in the strip of dark water surrounding the central ice cake. Arriving at dusk we had made a little night fire, lay down beside it and slept until dawn.

Arvo had awakened before I did and had a good cooking fire going but had gone down the shore a ways to fish. If we were to have coffee with our bacon and korpua I had to make a birchbark pail for we had no other one. Stripping off a square of the white bark (it strips easily in early spring) I folded its corners inward, turned up the sides and fastened them in place with split pegs made from a maple branch. For a bail or handle I used a peeled spruce root. Then filling it with lake water I hung the pail over the coals from a slanted pole jabbed into the ground.

You might think that the birchbark would catch on fire but it never does. So long as you keep the bark from direct contact with the flame the heat seems to go right through the bark into the water.

To make good camp coffee you throw a good handful of coffee into the water, let it boil two minutes, take it off the fire for one minute, then let it boil one minute more. No one has ever tasted better coffee than that cooked in a birchbark pail.

I also made two birchbark cups. They're easy to construct. You just roll a strip of birchbark into a cone, fold up its bottom half and pin it together with a peg that can also serve as a handle. Try it sometime.

Arvo had no pole. Instead he had fastened a three foot length of line to a big chunk of cedar with a large hook at the other end. Another line from that bobber lay in coils at his feet. Baiting the big hook with three or four large nightcrawlers he whirled the bobber around his head then let it fly far out into the water.

Almost immediately the cedar bobber began to jiggle. "Hey, Arvo," I yelled. "You've got a bite!"

"Naw," he answered. "Those are just little trout. They always bite first. When a big one sees their activity he will come to investigate and then wham!, down goes the whole big bobber and I've got him."

I was lacing together some peeled maple branches to make a grill for our bacon when suddenly Arvo let out a yell. Hand over hand he hauled in a very big fish. "A sloib," he shouted. "I've caught a sloib!"

I'd never heard that word before although I often have in recent years. It means a whopper. It has been used to refer not only to designate a big fish but to a pancake, a buck and even to a baby in the Upper Peninsula of Michigan. When I asked Arvo where he got the word he said it had just come to him. Not many people have been present at the birth of a new word. Anyway, it's a good one. After we roasted that sloib of a trout over the coals I caught some sloibs myself but none so large as Arvo's.

Well that was the memory and back to the present. Since I can have only one slice of bacon each week I like to have it thick and fried slowly and thoroughly so I use slab bacon only. I grinned as I put the slab on the back of a heavy wooden plaque that had been presented to me long before by Governor Romney because on the other side are the words "Michigan Frontiersman of the Year: Charles Van Riper." That's Cully Gage's alias. When I wrote my first Northwoods Reader I used a pen name and changed a lot of names and places fearing I might be sued by the descendants of the zany characters I wrote about. I needn't have worried because they felt flattered instead of being upset. "Cully" came from the Finnish word Kalla for Karl or Charles and Gage is my middle name and my mother's name. Everyone called me Cully when I was a boy and so did my wife and close friends. So much for that.

I grinned because I was remembering how Jim Miller, president of our university, reacted when I told him that I wouldn't accept it, that such honors always embarrassed me, that I was small potatoes and few in the hill and that I just didn't believe in honors. "Ever hear of the man who married for honor?" I asked jestingly. "He got on 'er."

That made him mad. "Van Riper," he said, "You'll damned well accept it. No matter how you feel, the university will benefit from the publicity. Tell you what I'll do. I'll drive you over to Detroit to the Economic Club luncheon where the presentation will be made, then drive you up to the Pere Marquette River, show you the biggest brown trout you've ever seen and let you flyfish for him." So I gave in and as a result got a fine cutting board for my bacon even if I didn't catch that trout.

All through breakfast and for some time afterward I got to thinking about honors and recognition and fame and how so many people hunger for them. What folly that is. Fame is for fruitflies. No matter how great our achievements we'll soon be forgotten. The life of our universe is measured in billions of light years and our little lives wink out like the sparks from a campfire. No, I've never worked to be famous or for the applause of others. Nuts to honors.

Nor have I beat myself to acquire possessions although they have come to me incidentally. I own an eighty acre farm in the middle of the city of Portage and more land in my beloved Upper Peninsula where I have my cabins but so what? How much do these amount to when you think of the immensity of space?

Specks, we are, tiny insignificant specks in time and space.

As I munched my toast I recalled how small my farm looked when I took my first hot air balloon ride at the age of eighty. From that basket floating lazily high in the sky, it was no bigger than a postage stamp. Yet there in the balloon I was the same size I'd always been. My house down there was just a tiny spot. How come I wasn't?

One of the real rewards of growing very old is that you have the time for watching your thoughts unfold and no guilt about doing so. Though you know there aren't many leaves left on your calendar, for the moment you have the feeling that you can spend your minutes any way you wish.

"Hey" I thought, "Even though you're just a point at the intersection of the two infinitely long lines of time and space, you can erect a perpendicular at that point, the perpendicular pronoun 'I' and that perpendicular can grow very tall. Yes, that's me. I'm not just a speck. I'm a perpendicular and the units of that perpendicular are the impacts for good that I have accomplished in my short lifetime. That's the measure of a man, not his possessions or fame. After a rough beginning I made my life into a shining thing by helping so many other poor devils down in the swamp of despair. Pioneering the new profession of speech pathology gave me the opportunity to grow tall and I'm lucky to have had that chance. No, I'm not insignificant.   I'm no speck.   I'm a perpendicular."

I found myself getting excited. I always do when I am doing some new thinking. "What is in that perpendicular?" I asked myself and the answer came immediately. It's the impact for good that we have on others. Every time we help another person, or make the world a bit more beautiful,we add a unit to our perpendicular of significance. And every time we hurt or create some ugliness we subtract from it. I've been fortunate in having had the opportunity to help a lot of poor devils who possessed tangled tongues and every time I did I grew a bit taller. No, I was no tiny speck.

Suddenly my train of thought braked to a halt. Once again my heart was going berserk, racing, and skipping. I knew it wasn't another bout of congestive heart failure because there was no gasping for air or hard coughing. It was probably another episode of ventricular tachycardia which is bad enough. Thanks to medication I have been free from it for a long time but its threat is always there and you can die from that too if fibrillation occurs. But I wasn't too worried until the condition persisted and sweat broke out all over me. Sometimes if I cough hard or bang my chest with my fist it will cease but not this time. So in desperation I took another quinidex and tucked a nitroglycerin pill under my tongue. Soon I sensed the familiar electric taste and a bit later the slower, and more regular thumping of the pulse in my forehead which usually means I'm coming out of it. Not so! The irregularity returned. Feeling that I was extremely tense and that the tension might be contributing to the tachycardia,   I decided to try the deep relaxation methods I'd learned from Kima, a wise and holy man from India. Occasionally it had helped me before. The procedure is this: 1. Greatly prolong each exhalation; 2. Roll your eyeballs upward under your eyelids, and 3. Let all your body slump. After about ten minutes of this Hindu relaxation the heart was beating smoothly again but I was exhausted. Phew!

Lord, I thought, even thinking can be dangerous. I had let myself become too excited. Well, I'd again learned something new about my limits.

Knowing it would be wise to be quiet for a time but reluctant to lie down lest I start thinking again, I went to my study and got an old book I'd written years before that had a tale about Kima in it, about the man from India who had taught me his way of relaxing under stress.

This is the essence of his story.

In 1932, during the depth of the great depression I was at the University of Iowa getting my doctorate in clinical psychology. With very little money I was existing on peanut butter and day old bread from a local bakery until I finally got an assistantship helping Dr. Travis in the laboratory where he was doing pioneer work in recording brain waves. While it only paid fifty dollars a month that was quite sufficient for all my needs and I was shocked when one day he told me he was relieving me of all my duties. "No," he said when he saw my fallen face, "You're not fired. I"ve just got another project for you - to photograph the soul."

Grinning, he explained that his dean had told him that a very important scholar from India had arrived on campus and wanted to know more about those brain waves, that he hoped thereby to see the mind or soul in action and to have it photographed. "He's nuts of course," Dr. Travis said, "but I'm assigning the project to you. Just keep him out of my hair."

Kima was a short man of about sixty years but had the unfurrowed face of a boy. "For many years I have sought to see my soul," he told me, "and now I have heard that you of the Western world have found a way of showing the brain in action. This I must see, my son." When I was about to hook the electrodes on his head however, he said no and that I should demonstrate it on another person first.

So I hooked up a friend and showed him the action currents on the screen, the alpha and beta waves and all the jumbled rest of them. Of course they made no sense to him because all they showed was consciousness, that the brain was alive.

"I must see pure thought," Kima said. My own thoughts weren't very pure at the moment but I said I'd have to think about it. At last I came up with a possible solution. Kima had told me that the soul is most active when the person is inactive but imagining, so I built an apparatus consisting of an arm chair and a board to which a person's arm could be strapped. "We'll sit the subject in the chair," I said, "then compare the brain waves when he voluntarily lifts the board, when the board is lifted for him by this rope and pulley, and finally when he is just imagining that he's lifting the board. By seeing the difference in the brain waves when he is just imagining we should come pretty close to finding what you want." Kima agreed and was excited when I put Travis's pretty secretary in the contraption and hooked on the electrodes.

She lifted her arm, I lifted her arm (and wished it were her leg), and she just imagined lifting it as the camera rolled. Alas, when I developed the film there wasn't a damned bit of difference between any of the recordings.

"I must meditate upon this thing," said Kima.

The next day when he returned he had the solution. "We failed," he said, "because you Americans are too tense and that tension masks the pure thought of imagining. I must teach you how to relax." I gathered some other graduate students and Kima trained us for several days before attempting the experiment again.

Unfortunately, that failed too and I know why. It was Kima's third step, the one where we also had to visualize existence as a whole while contemplating our navels. All of us mastered prolonging our exhalations and rolling our eyeballs up under our eyelids but every time we contemplated our navels our eyeballs went down. Kima was disappointed and so was I. Nevertheless, I have used his first two steps often since and was usually successful. And this morning I did so again.

By the time I had finished reading about Kima I was feeling pretty good so I decided to take my usual morning walk in my park. I've always enjoyed walking and in my youth I hiked all over many of the wilderness areas of the Upper Peninsula. Not any more! My diabetes led to neuropathy in my legs and though last year I had arterial by-pass surgery on them every step I take hurts. Nevertheless I walk all I can and am happy I don't have to use a cane as I did for some months. How I hated that damned cane even though it was a beautiful shillely I'd bought in Ireland. It always made me feel old and despite my years I rarely do unless reminded.

So, with a bit of wincing, I walked down the lane behind the old barn into my park. When I bought the farm about fifty years ago there was a little four acre barren field there that had been used as a holding place for dairy cattle. Foolishly I thought that manure from years of cows would have made it fertile so I planted it to corn. Only a few straggly stalks appeared and they were as stunted as the weeds. The ground turned out to be mainly hard pan clay with only an inch of topsoil on it. How my wife snorted when I told her I would make that field into a park, into my own little bit of the U.P.

But I did! The next spring I plowed the whole field and sowed it to sweet clover with lots of fertilizer, plowed that under and sowed a crop of buckwheat, again plowed that under and in the fall I put in a cover crop of rye. After three years of that rotation the soil was soft and mellow and I could begin to plant the bushes and trees of the U.P.

First I planted hundreds of seedling spruce, balsam, and various kinds of pines, then some poplars and birch. Every summer I brought back from my cabin on the Van Riper Lakes large rocks covered with moss, ferns or groundpine. Arbutus, however refused to be transplanted. Year after year I tried but it always withered and died. I guess it didn't want to live Down Below any more than I did. Two hazelnut bushes flourished but two tamaracks did not. I did manage to bring back some U.P. flowers that have done very well: trilliums, jack in the pulpits, adder's tongues, violets and Dutchman's breeches.

As I walked through the park today I was again amazed to see how tall those trees had grown. The firs and pines were at least fifty feet tall and the ground beneath them was covered by a thick mat of brown needles. To rest my legs I lay down on them for some time listening to the wind in the branches as I'd done so often in my beloved homeland. For a few moments I was again a boy in the forest.

Then I went over to the little blue pool in the pines. Compared to my sparkling lakes north of Tioga it is just a trivial gesture but it's water and I couldn't have my bit of the U.P. without some. I fill the pool with a three hundred foot hidden hose from the barn and let the water flow over the bordering rocks just to hear the familiar sound. Often I sit hidden back from it to watch the animals come there to drink at dusk. I've seen raccoons, possum, rabbits, squirrels and occasionally deer. My farm is about the only free space where animals can live out their days, surrounded as it is by subdivisions of expensive houses.

This morning however there were no animals but a pheasant flushed from the tangle beyond the pool. I've let part of my park grow up to underbrush so my visitors can hide.

Then I followed the little path through the rest of the firs to the back gate of my park and stood there overlooking my meadows. After a disastrous experience trying to grow wheat in my back forty acres I've just let the land go fallow. The land is hilly and rolling and long grass covered all of it except for my woodlot and the wild cherry and other trees that have appeared. It's a lovely spot and for years I've walked it every day and for a moment I was tempted to do it again.

I didn't, knowing it would be enough just to walk back to the house but I promised myself I'd come back that afternoon to see if the kids from the big houses beyond the boundary trees had been building shacks again. They do so every year and sometimes build fires that have threatened my park. When I find such a shack I try to visit it when the kids are there, show them how to build a firepit, tell them tales of Pete Halfshoes, my boyhood Indian friend, and give them a handful of marshmallows to roast.

Getting back to the house yard sure wore me out so I sat for a time on the bench that encircles the biggest of my large oak trees. How often my wife and I have sat there watching the sun go down over the west fields! After some good memories I re-entered the house.

There I lay down on the davenport and had almost dozed off when the phone rang. Ach! It was Patrick Mulligan from a little town in Illinois. He said that he had just preached his last sermon before retiring and wanted to thank me again for curing his stuttering. He said he was thinking of coming to see me to tell me about all the souls he had saved and perhaps to save my own. I firmly said no, that I'd had a heart failure and was seeing no visitors, I just couldn't bear the thought of seeing him on his knees before me praying for my benighted soul. Finally I convinced him or hoped I had.

I couldn't help remembering that Pat had come to me in 1953 stuttering very severely with many gasps and head jerks. For some years he had worked on an oil drilling crew in Oklahoma but had become a born again Christian with a calling to preach the gospel according to Saint Patrick. He'd had little schooling but could read and write even if he couldn't talk.

Respecting his sincerity and high motivation, although I felt the prognosis was very poor, I started to teach him how to change and modify his stuttering so he could be fluent enough to preach. To my surprise Pat progressed rapidly and within the year he was remarkably fluent. When he left on his mission I confess I felt relieved. How many hours I had spent with him reading the Bible, praying and preaching and resisting his efforts to convert me! For some years thereafter Pat visited me to report on his missionary progress and to save my bloody soul. A self ordained minister, he had built a small church of concrete blocks with his own hands in a farm community and gradually gathered a little congregation to hear his impassioned sermons. No small achievement, that! In a way I envied his simple faith in God and the hereafter.

In my long life I've seen how much strength such a faith has given others in deep trouble. One of them was my wife's Aunt Nell who spent a week with us when she was almost eighty. She had the unwrinkled face of an angel and serenity radiated from it. All of us felt it, even my children. I knew that she'd had a miserable and tragic life with a husband who was one of the nastiest, cruelest men I've ever known. For years they'd existed in abject poverty. One son had committed suicide; another was a scoundrel. And yet Aunt Nell was a saint, a very happy beautiful person. How had she been able to surmount all those difficulties and have such peace? When I finally asked her, she said, "Every morning when I wake up I ask the Lord what wonderful things He has in store for me and, you know, He has never once disappointed me." I've worked with cancer victims who had lost their tongues or vocal cords who had that same faith and always I've marveled at their courage and peace of mind.

I have long sought that faith. It would be good to have it now but I'm an agnostic like my father except that I doubt my doubts and he never did. Though he never flaunted his scepticism and agreed with my devout mother that I should go to Sunday School and church, he never attended. He said he'd lost his faith in medical school and that religion, like most of medicine, was largely humbug. Yet his best friend was Father Hassel, our old Catholic priest, with whom he played a weekly game of chess over a small glass of whiskey and a cigar. Once I heard them arguing about religion and hearing the priest say, "Doctor, you're an old fraud. You're more religious than anyone I know. You've always sacrificed yourself for others. God works his wonders in many mysterious ways and you, sir, have been his instrument whether you know it or not." Others have said the same about me.

And I've often had truly religious experiences - though not in church. I love the old hymns and the liturgy but most of the sermons have always turned me off. The forest is my temple and I've had some peak experiences therein during which I found myself caught up in a power far greater than myself. In The Last Northwoods Reader there is a story called Campfires which describes one such incident.

The Bench

When my legs finally stopped hurting I went outside to the old barn to chop some wood for the evening fire. Knowing from past experience that I had to be careful, I started on a chunk of cedar I'd brought back from the U.P. Splitting cedar is always enjoyable and easy. You "read" the end of the chunk to see just where to hit and then, by angling the blade at the last moment, the slab breaks away cleanly with one swipe. So I made an armful of kindling without any ill effects. I knew I should have quit right then but a nice clean chunk of oak was so inviting I got the heavy maul and whopped it a good one, breaking it in half. Oops! I felt the old heaviness in my chest and quit immediately, then sat on the bench in the sun humming "Lazy bones, sitting in the sun. How you gonna get your day's work done, sitting in the noonday sun?" Now my voice is only good for cooling soup but I sang anyway. Ours was always a singing family. All of us always sang at the dining table between the main meal and dessert. Sitting there on the bench I could almost hear the bright voices of my children singing Harvest Moon, Home on the Range or that one about the pufferbellies. How did it go? Oh yes, "Down by the station/ early in the morning/ see the little pufferbellies all in a row/ Hear the stationmaster blow his little whistle/ Pop Pop. Toot Toot/ Away we go." Always my wife was singing the old songs and doing little dance steps as she cooked or did the dishes and she could always harmonize wonderfully too. Oh well, that was long ago—but not too far away.

Getting up from the bench I gathered asters and chrysanthemums for the house. Milove always loved flowers and I've kept some fresh ones in her bedroom ever since she died.

Those I put in her vase were Yoshiko's mums, special ones. Yoshiko Ohashi was the stuttering daughter of a prominent Japanese government official and when she came to me for therapy she proved to be one of my most difficult patients. I just couldn't know her feelings because her body language was so different. When that oriental mask of a face smiled it was not with amusement but rather embarrassment. When she giggled, she was angry. Moreover she fought me tooth and nail, sabotaging the assignments I gave her and often just refusing to cooperate in anyway. I felt she hated me. Was she reacting to me as though I were a rejecting father figure? I didn't know but it was obvious that I was failing and would have no possible chance of helping her. Finally she stopped coming for therapy although she continued her academic studies in speech pathology at our university.

I decided that if I were to help her I just had to know more about the Japanese so for several months I immersed myself in Japanese art, literature, history and culture, reading everything in our library that I could. It was in itself a fascinating and rewarding experience and I found some important new insights. Evidently the Japanese penalized the deviant individual much more that we did. In one of their famous plays, the Domo Mata, a famous painter was urged by his wife to commit suicide because of his shameful speech. I learned that a frustrated stutterer had deliberately burned down one of their most sacred shrines, the

Temple of the Golden Pavilion, much to the shock and anger of the whole nation. In one of their books I read about a man who said that every time he stuttered a hundred of his ancestors turned in their graves with revulsion. It became obvious that I had asked Yoshiko to confront her disorder before she could possible tolerate doing so. Somehow I had to desensitize her to her stuttering before we could make any headway.

I sought her out and we began therapy again, this time with much more success and she returned to Japan fluent enough to become an instructor in speech pathology at one of their universities. Then some years later when she wrote that she was returning to see me and thank me I asked her to bring some seeds of their national flower, the chrysanthemum.

She came but not with seeds. Instead she brought some cuttings, hiding them in her bra to escape customs. I planted them by the windmill and one of them that survived has bloomed gloriously ever since. It was some of Yoshiko's mums that I put on Milove's bedside table.

It was now time to get on my exercycle (a stationary bicycle) on my daily ride to the Upper Peninsula - or so I pretend. I travel on it one or two miles each day and at present I'm a few miles north of Grand Rapids. By March I will be in Cadillac, in two months I'll be crossing The Bridge and by June I'll be at my lakes. I hope the arbutus will still be blooming on the north side of the hills.

As always, the morning had passed swiftly and it was time to take my mandatory nap. To make it more tolerable I play classical music on my big stereo and this time I chose a Beethoven Symphony. For a long time I followed the familiar music but then dozed off, not awakening until the music stopped.

Refreshed, I made myself some soup and a sandwich and after some self debate about riding down on my garden tractor I decided to walk to the mailbox. My 132 year old farmhouse sits on a little hill and there are 239 double steps that I must take to get to it, each of which will hurt me because, due to my diabetic neuropathy, I have only half the circulation in my legs that I should have. The diabetes is now under control by a strict diet and glycotrol but the neuropathy still remains. Once on the way down and twice on the way back I had to rest but the effort was worth it because there was a lot of good mail, much of it addressed to Cully Gage. I sure love those letters from my readers and answer most of them. Impact again! Back in the house I read a few of them, then saved the others until later.

Tired of sitting and reluctant to miss any of that fine day, I went to the north garden to dig a few potatoes. I did so with anticipation because for forty years I have tried to grow The Perfect Potato. Let others seek to grow the perfect rose or dahlia or orchid. My goal has been to take a lowly clod of a vegetable and make it into a shining thing as I've done with some human clods, including myself.

People have asked me how I would know if I'd grown one even if I did. I tell them that I would know. It would be unblemished, have closed or sleeping eyes and be very large. Eight years ago I grew a ten inch one that looked so perfect I almost had it bronzed. Although I kept it on my fireplace mantel until it got soft and wrinkled I knew that on its underside there was a flaw. So my quest has continued.

This year, knowing that my time was getting short, I had planted the potatoes with special care. Two wide and deep trenches had been filled with a mixture of compost, peat moss and rich earth before I laid down the cut seed tubers and covered them with bone meal and more compost. All summer I had weeded and watered the patch carefully. The vines had been thick, and heavy with flowers but now they were brown and shriveled. It was time to see if I had fulfilled my dream.

Getting a spade from the old horse stall which was now my garden room I went over to the potato patch but rested a while on a nail keg before starting to dig. Again more memories filled my head. That potato patch had once been my pigpen and had held an inverted V-shaped pig house in which my children played happily until their mother discovered them. She told me to get rid of the structure but instead I bought two month-old pigs naming them Cornelius and George after two of our university deans who had given me trouble.

How I enjoyed those little buggers! They'd see me coming with a pail of slop and race around the pen oinking to high heaven, and after they grew into huge hogs they loved the hard cider I mixed with their mash. Like me, they also loved flowers, especially those in my wife's house beds. Time after time I would have to coax them back to the pen they'd tunneled under and then try to repair the fence. Pigs are smart animals, smarter about fences than I was.

Sitting there in their old haunts I remembered the time I came home from a long speaking trip to find my wife so livid with fury she wouldn't even kiss me. "You'll have to get rid of those damned pigs or you'll be rid of me!" With fury she told about how those pigs of mine had broken out again and cleaned out all her lovely annuals, how she'd gone out in her nightgown to chase them away and they wouldn't chase. Wow! Was she mad. And beautiful too with her brown eyes flashing lightning! When I couldn't keep my face straight, visualizing that scene, she sure let me have it.

In any happy marriage there are times when a man has to do battle but this was not one of them. At first I thought of having Dean George and Dean Cornelius butchered and processed for our freezer but I knew that would create many future difficulties, that neither she nor my children would eat a bit of them. So I sold my beloved hogs and every time we had oatmeal for breakfast, or hamburger for dinner I mourned the loss of bacon and sausage and chops and roasts. Most of all I missed the chance to munch on my academic enemies but there was peace in the vale.

Still smiling at that memory I began to dig the potatoes, pausing after each hill to sit for a time on the nail keg. Oh, it was going to be a fine crop, the first hill yielding fourteen spuds, most of them big ones. They were clean, white and noble. Two of them were more than eight inches long so I dug three more hills with eagerness, but The Perfect Potato was not among them. No matter! There were thirty six hills still to be dug and surely in one of them I would find it. How I wanted to keep on digging but sensibly I did not. I hate being sensible. Laying all I'd dug on a blue tarp to dry I returned to the house.

One of the consequences of congestive heart failure, as my doctor told me, is deep fatigue after very little effort. "When you feel it, lie down whether you want to or not."   So I did, remembering how in Tioga shortly after the beginning of school the boys were excused to help in the potato harvest. I remembered working on John Delongchamp's farm from six to six, going along the rows of potatoes that had been dug, sorting them and putting the good ones into burlap bags. We also put the small ones in piles and set aside the sloibs. These Jumbos were the really big ones, up to a foot long. Delongchamp saved these for the county fair or for special customers. Once he gave my father a bushel of those monsters and I recall that for one dinner meal my mother baked just one of them for the whole family. Some Jumbos had a cavity within them but this one did not. I've never seen potatoes like those since.   Dad said that Delongchamp grew them in virgin sod without manure or fertilizer - just U.P. sunshine and rain from Lake Superior.

Next I read the rest of my mail and wrote some letters, one to a little boy who said his teacher had read some of my stories to his class. He liked the ones about me and Mullu and Fisheye and the tricks we played in school but his favorite was the one about the bat in the hat. Finally I wrote one to a man who said he'd been hunting for Tioga for three summers and where the hell was it anyway? Tioga was really Champion, I wrote, and Lake Tioga was Lake Michigamme. Van Riper State Park was named after my father who started it because one day when he went there to go swimming and had to change his clothes in some bushes some little Finn kids had embarrassed him by chanting "Look at Doctor's big white ass! Look at Doctor's big white ass." My father got the township to put up some dressing rooms and rake out the beach, took one more swim and never went back there again.

Noticing that the battered old copper boiler that holds my firewood was empty I went out to the barn to get the garden tractor and cart to haul the wood for the evening fire and at the same time to fetch the evening paper from the mailbox. As I rode back up the lane I glanced at the headlines. War in the Persian Gulf, homicides, rape. I wouldn't read it till morning. Hell, I wouldn't even read it then so I rolled the sheets into cylinders, placed them on the grate, laid the apple small wood and an oak chunk on them and started the evening fire.

It was time to see if I could have whiskey for Happy Hour so I went into my study to test my blood sugar. Diabetics have to be careful about alcohol. Pricking my forefinger with the lancet, I put the drop of blood on the test tape, closed the instrument's door and waited while the display said testing, testing, until it wrote 127. Good! No Diet Cola tonight. The blood sugar was well within the 80-140 range of normality.

Old men need to pamper themselves a little so I buy good scotch, Chivas Regal or Glenn Fiddich, for my two fingers of whiskey in a tin cup I'd brought back from the old cabin. Whiskey somehow always tastes better from a tin cup. I wished I had water from my big spring up there but because I still have my own well at least I don't spoil it with the hint of chlorine that pollutes city water. Because I sip it very slowly, one cup usually lasts a long time beside the fire at Happy Hour.

I love that hour and so did Milove. We'd sit and share with each other the happenings of the day. It was always good talk, sometimes crazy talk. Even now, especially on a day when I 've heard no human voice, I converse aloud with her knowing just how she would respond to my nonsense .   Though her picture is on the TV it seems as though she is sitting next to me in her blue chair. "I 'm only a smile away," she wrote on an Indian slate at the cabin before she died. I smile a lot at Happy Hour .

Then it was time to make supper . Though I wasn't hungry I know I must not skip a meal because of the diabetes, so I cut one of my acorn squash in half, filled the cavity with bits of link sausage, and put it in the oven to bake. That, with milk, bread and an apple would be my evening meal . While it was cooking I thought of a tale that I had started to write but had never finished. Where the devil was it? I searched my messy study and finally found it on top of the encyclopedia. It was fun reading and the need to finish it was so strong I went to the typewriter after supper and did so. Here it is:

Aunt Lizzie's Downfall

Even roses wither and age by the clock but that didn't seem true of Aunt Lizzie Compton, Tioga's gossip and trouble maker. Daily she made her rounds down our hill street and on the side roads to Frenchtown and Finntown. Only the worst blizzards kept her inside. Physically she changed little as she aged. Her step and her voice were strong, the latter too strong because Annie, our long suffering organist, finally gave our new preacher an ultimatum.

"Mr. Jones," she said, "You've got to get Aunt Lizzie out of the choir or I'm quitting. For twenty years she has tortured my ears and those of your congregation. She fancies herself quite a soprano but she's never been able to hit the high notes fair and square; she flats them and screeches them instead. I've tried for a long time to cover them up by playing the organ louder but my feet get tired from all that pumping. What's worse is that lately she's lost the top part of the range she had. She doesn't know that, of course, but everyone else does. Her lower notes are ok but oh she murders those high ones. I feel them in my spine! I tell you it's Aunt Lizzie or me and you' ll not find another organist in town." The Reverend Jones said he'd see what could be done.

So the next day he called a meeting of the church board and found that all its members agreed with Annie. It was high time that Aunt Lizzie stepped down. "But who is to grab that wildcat by the tail?" asked one board member. Most of them had felt the bite of Aunt Lizzie's tongue at one time or another. "You're the preacher, " they said . "That ' s your job . "

Feeling sorry for the preacher, Annie suggested that he circulate a petition and use it if Aunt Lizzie refused to cooperate, so that is what the preacher did. The only dissenter who refused to sign was old Andy Anderson. "Hell ," he said, "The only reason I go to church is to hear the old gal screech and watch the people try to keep their fingers out of their ears."

Thinking it was just a pastoral visit, Aunt Lizzie made the preacher a cup of tea the next afternoon when he called at her house, but when he gently told her that she should let a younger singer take her place in the choir she took it away from him.

"Preacher," she said, "I'll do no such thing. I can sing as

well as I ever could. I'll have you know that I started your choir thirty years ago. I bought the robes, much of the music and helped pay for the organ." She was getting madder by the moment. "Who puts a whole dollar in your collection plate each Sunday? Who makes the best cake for your cake sales? Who teaches your Sunday School when the regular teacher gets sick? Of all the nerve! No, I say, No, no, no!" When the preacher told her of Annie's ultimatum Aunt Lizzie said she'd play the organ herself and sing soprano too. Fearing that soon she'd be scratching his eyes out, the preacher handed her the petition and fled with her final words ringing in his ears: "I'll be there next Sunday, preacher, and I'll be singing soprano in the choir!"

As you can imagine, the news of Aunt Lizzie's firing traveled like wildfire throughout Tioga. As she made her daily rounds, Aunt Lizzie for the first time found herself on the defensive. "Hey, I hear they kicked you out of the choir." "You aren't going to let them do that to you, are you Aunt Lizzie, without a fight?" "I hear they've moved Thirza Lowe up from contralto to soprano and that Bill Trevarrow will be singing tenor. Funny choir, that will be, with three men and only one female voice!'

Wow! That news sure made Aunt Lizzie furious. "You mean they're picking that saloon singer in my place?" she shouted incredulously, "I won't stand for it! " Yes, they told her, Bill is going to be in the new choir and they're practicing in the preachers' house every evening.

Although it was a fine summer day the church was full that next Sunday morning. Our people knew that Aunt Lizzie would put up a battle and when they saw her going down the street wearing her choir robe they knew the fireworks would soon begin.

Their expectations were fulfilled. Up into the choir loft strode Aunt Lizzie to join the three men and Thirza. When the preacher went over to persuade her to leave she shouted NO in such a loud voice the whole congregation gasped. Annie gave the organ a big blast and left her bench to sit in the front row to see what would happen, and soon the other members of the choir followed her. There was Aunt Lizzie up there alone but undaunted.

She held up her hand for silence and sure got it. "Our first hymn this morning will be The Old Rugged Cross, she announced. "I shall sing the first verse while accompanying myself on the organ and you will then join in on the second which you will find on page 64." Hers was the voice of command and many people did open their hymn books to that page.

At first the congregation was stunned but by the time Aunt Lizzie had finished that first verse all hell broke loose.. "No, no!" they yelled. "Step down, Lizzie! We want the new choir. This is our church, not yours. Down, down!" Nothing so exciting had happened in Tioga since Bridget Murphy's pig fell in the well.

Trying to maintain the holiness of the sanctuary in all that commotion, the preacher went over to Charlie Olafson, our town constable, and whispered something in his ear. Up got the big man from his pew and striding up to the choir loft he picked up Aunt Lizzie and carried her to a back pew despite her struggles, then sat beside her.

The new choir made its way back to the loft; Annie returned to the organ bench, and the preacher to the pulpit. "Friends," he said. "I deeply regret the disturbance and am sorry it occurred. Mrs. Compton has done many good works in this church and I'm sorry she has been hurt. The text for my sermon this morning comes from Luke 10, verse 5. It is 'Peace to this house.' But first let us listen to our new choir's first selection." Annie belted out a triumphant fanfare and the three men and Thirza sang a hymn whose title I've forgotten but it was one of those with a lot of the high notes that Aunt Liz loved.

And in that back pew Aunt Lizzie sang with them. Loud and clear, she sang and way off key on those high notes until Charlie put a fat hand over her mouth.

She bit that hand right to the bone and the words that Charlie uttered were not those usually heard in the house of the Lord. Dead silence! Charlie picked up Aunt Lizzie, slung her over his shoulder, and carried her up to the steel cage in our Town Hall that served as the jail. "You'll be here till morning, Lizzie," he said, "and then I'll decide whether to have you arraigned before the justice of the peace for assault and battery upon an officer of the law. So shut up!"

That afternoon some of us kids were peering through the windows of the town hall to enjoy her shaking her fist at us when Charlie came and let her out. She was not at all contrite and we couldn't help admiring her spirit. Nothing could conquer Aunt Lizzie.

And nothing did. Wiser heads worked out a compromise because they felt sorry for her. After all, she'd done a lot for the church for many years and didn't really know how off key she sang. So they moved Thirza up to sing soprano and asked Aunt Lizzie to be the contralto. It worked out fine. Peace in the valley and peace on the hill came to Tioga and everyone lived happily ever after. Or should have!

Well, that done I went to bed. It had been a good day.

DAY TWO

I awoke a bit later than usual probably because at three o'clock I'd gone downstairs to limber up my hurting legs on my exercycle. It had helped and I'd gone back to sleep swiftly but this morning they were aching again so I began to exercise them and my toes before I even got out of bed to get the circulation going. Diabetics develop a neuropathy that causes numbness in the extremities and that has happened to me. Once I stepped on a thumbtack before I went to bed and it was there next morning when I found it while taking a bath. Exercising my toes doesn't eliminate the numbness but it may prevent the severe ulcers that plagued me last year. So I wiggle my toes a lot every morning.

I've set myself a quota of thirty wiggles and was half through doing them when I got mad. I was in a rut, living my hours and days in the same way. I was a damned robot! I've always enjoyed being a bit different and unpredictable. I like to do the unexpected, to explore new experiences, to take crazy chances and here I was, just a laboratory rat, running the same maze day after day. Furious with myself, I vowed that this new day would be different.

Therefore I got out of bed on the left side rather than the right where I usually slept and I exercised those toes by dancing on them down to the bathroom to the tune of Waltzing Matilda and I put on a bright red shirt and red socks to complete a costume that was decidedly different from that which I usually wear. Felt like a bull fighter.

Instead of greeting the world with my customary hello, I rang the old bell instead to greet the day. Once again I was glad I'd not sold the farm to those beady eyed developers who pester me. I enjoy the feeling of isolation, to be able to do my Dance of the Wild Cucumber under the full moon or to ring that bell when I want to without worrying about my neighbors.

Washing out an old black jug I'd found in a lumber camp up north I filled it with cider and drank it from the jug. Now for a different breakfast, not the usual oatmeal or bran flakes, toast and coffee. Peacock tongues? There weren't any in the cupboard but I did find a string of Upper Peninsula mushrooms my wife had long before dried by hanging them from our cabin window frame. Were they still good? I didn't know but I made them into an omelet anyway. Instead of using my automatic coffee maker I made a pot of boiled coffee and suddenly thought of the best cup of coffee I've ever tasted, the one I had on the Bayou de la Fange in Louisiana many years ago.

I was in Louisiana to conduct a week-long seminar in stuttering for the speech therapists in that area. The group was a large one, perhaps a hundred or more but they were hungry to learn and the days passed swiftly. Most of them were young and attractive but I especially noticed one of them, a white haired old lady, who sat in the back row and took down every word I said. At the end of the Thursday session she came up and introduced herself.

She was not a speech therapist, she said, but had come to hear me in the hope that she could help her forty year old son, Raoul, who stuttered and who had isolated himself on their plantation since quitting high school at sixteen. She told me Raoul talked as little as possible to anyone, spent his days in his room listening to the radio or reading or wandering in the swamp. Perhaps if he saw me and heard me, another person who had stuttered and became fluent, he might get some hope and stop being such a hermit. She said she hesitated to ask, but could I, would I come to their home to see Raoul? She warned me he might refuse to come downstairs or refuse to speak to me, but would I please come. Of course I said yes.

Her chauffeur picked me up that afternoon and drove me to a landing on the Bayou de la Fange where we took a launch to the plantation. The driver explained that it was easier that way because of the muddy roads and that Mme. F. thought I would enjoy the boat ride. I certainly did. The trees hung heavy with moss, there were strange shrubs in full bloom, and birds sang everywhere.

The house was very old and very beautiful. Mme. F. welcomed me graciously and showed me a huge book of historic homes in which the house was pictured. The book said it had been built in the days of Napoleon and that the roof tiles had come from France in a sailing ship. Both she and her husband were of French descent, very proud to be Creoles. He was a consulting engineer specializing in the construction of sugar refineries and soon to retire. He would be joining us later, she said. She led me through a large drawing room into a little alcove overlooking a beautiful garden and excused herself. "I must persuade Raoul to come down if I can." I suggested that she should let us be by ourselves if he did show up and she agreed.

More than twenty minutes elapsed before Raoul appeared and sat down. A large man, very fat, he wouldn't shake hands when we were introduced. At first I did almost all the talking, telling of my own experiences as a stutterer and demonstrating that I knew his feelings about his disorder. I showed Raoul how I used to stutter and also how fluent I had become. I verbalized the joys of being freed from a tangled tongue. No hard sell, of course, just a calm, almost casual presentation of factual material.

Throughout the long soliloquy, and that is what it was because Raoul didn't say a word, I was watching his body language intently. At first it seemed to reflect complete indifference, then some flickers of attention, then some alarm, and finally some real interest. When these signals appeared, I told him I wasn't there to try to get him to undertake any therapy, that I had come only because of his mother's concern, and because he probably needed some hope. It was only then that he began to talk.

"I know," Raoul said. "My mother is worrying about what will happen to me when she and my father die and I am left here alone. They are getting old, yes." He didn't stutter frequently or severely as he said this and had only one hard blocking. He told me that he wasn't worried because he lived only one day at a time. He was never bored because his hobby was baseball. Although he had never seen a professional game, Raoul knew the batting averages of players on several baseball teams and followed them closely on the radio and in the newspapers. He made predictions and bets with himself on the outcomes of the games. Yes, it was almost an obsession but it passed the time away and when there was no baseball he hunted and fished. Why go out into the evil world and have to talk and suffer? Here he was safe and happy. "Glad to have met you." He shook hands with me, smiled and left. I lit my pipe and wiped my brow.

When his mother came in she took one look at my face and knew. "Ah, mon fils," she said, patting my arm. "It was a long chance and I know you tried. Raoul, he has lived this way too long. Now you must meet my husband and share our pleasantness." A maid came in with sweets and tiny eggshell thin cups. "These are from old France," she said, "and now you must know the coffee of that time." The maid put a bit of very black coffee in each fragile cup, then a teaspoon of boiling water over it, then another teaspoon of boiling water and so on until the tiny cup was almost full. Then brown sugar and thick cream were added. It indeed was the best coffee I've ever tasted. Raoul's father, a gay spirit, joined us and had some too. No further mention of the son - just gaiety and civility. The father told tales of the Creoles and I told about the French Canadians of the forest village where I had spent my boyhood. We even knew and sang the same old song of the voyageurs:

"Oh ze wind she blo from ze nort,
And ze wind, she blo some more,
But you won't get drown on Lac Champlain
So long you stay on ze shore."

I don't know what happened to Raoul when his parents died and he had to leave that shore.

Still remembering that wonderful coffee I poured out the boiled coffee I'd made and started anew. Getting one of my wife's fragile Haviland china cups from the china closet I put a pan of water to boil as I fixed the omelet. Then I made my coffee as the maid in Louisiana had done. It was a fine breakfast but the coffee wasn't so good. Perhaps it was because I had to use Equal instead of the brown raw sugar, or the coffee itself didn't have that slight taste of chickory or because I had to use milk instead of thick cream. Anyway it was a different breakfast.

Rather than taking my customary walk in the park I rode the John Deere down the lane and into the meadows of my back fields. Around its perimeter I went, often having to dodge a young tree or two. Under a blowdown I discovered a new fox hole complete with paw print in the sand it had dug out. On the second hill I saw the oval flattened bed where a deer had slept. Two pheasants and three rabbits were sent scurrying. Down in the south valley I got off the tractor to look over my woodlot. Yes, there were many dead elms and some old wild cherry trees that should be sawed down. Returning along the west and north boundaries I saw the hint of autumn in the rose colored leaves of sassafras. Soon those fence rows would be aflame.

When I got back to the house I found I was very tired even though all I'd done was to sit and bounce. I felt like Samson must have felt after Delilah cut his hair, but it was good to lie down, a little old man in a big old house with sunshine streaming through the tall windows.

Yet I would rather have been barreling across those back fields in my ancient truck with my chain saw because I had a touch of the U.P. fall fever for making more wood for the winter. I was pretty sure I had enough stacked in the barn to last until spring but you never know. Perhaps we'd have a winter like that of 1946 when the drifts touched the farm bell and all my firewood was gone by the first of March. Oh nuts! I had enough and if I needed more I could buy it.

In the U.P. when I was a boy some of our men started making wood early in the spring. They'd go out on snowshoes and

31

cut down three or four big maples that they would cut up later in the summer. That way there'd be no sap in the trees and the wood could dry better. Most of us waited until July when the black flies, gnats and nosee-ums (big feel-ums) were gone. But when September came with its first hint of frost the wood fever flared again. We had to make it through the winter. "Got all yer wood made yet?" was a common greeting.

How the forest rang with the sound of crosscut saws and toppling trees in October! How vividly I recalled the sharp crack of the axe as it bit into the tree, the sight of our breath in the frosty air, the zing-zing of the saw, the smell of fresh sawdust. With a good partner on the other end of the long cross-cut saw the experience was very pleasant; with a bad one, it was not. "Dammit!" we would growl. "Don't mind yer riding the saw but quit dragging your feet!" Some real skill was involved. One had to pull hard but smoothly and without twisting the handle and on the return stroke you didn't push but merely guided the blade. Most of all, the two of us had to be in complete synchrony. With a well filed saw and sometimes a bit of kerosene on the blade the sawing could be almost effortless. Yes, it was fun making wood for the winter.

No one in Tioga ever seemed to have enough room in their barns or sheds to hold all the wood that had been cut and so each house usually had a woodpile outside. Some always stacked their wood by the outhouse in order that anyone going there to do his duty would remember to bring back a stick or two to the kitchen. Others used it for insulation, piling it around the foundations of their houses. A few made their woodpiles of split wood like igloos so the snow or rain wouldn't wet the inside of the pile. By deer season you could take the measure of a man by the looks of his woodpile.

Sometimes the fever became compulsive. Norman Bentti once had a pile of split wood higher than his two story house although his cellar and shed were full. People came from afar to admire Mount Bentti. Most of us made more wood than we really needed because it would always keep and besides it could always be given to someone in the village who might run out. We took care of each other in Tioga.

As I got off the davenport the obsession to live differently still had hold of me. How could I ride my exercycle on my way to the U.P. differently? Well, I could try to ride it backwards but, much to my surprise, that proved to be very difficult. My feet stuttered. They wanted to move in their accustomed way. When I pedaled slowly I could do it but reversals occurred at normal speeds. I managed to do only a half mile before giving up. Ruts were hard to break.

I then went out to tend my roses which had been neglected for some time because of the lush blooming of dahlias and chrysanthemums. Yes, they needed some tending but every bush was glorious with large blooms as they often are late in autumn. I grow fine roses though most visitors never see them because the rose bed is back of the old barn where many years of cow manure had been piled. They also grow well there because underneath the bed is a layer of the cinders and cobblestones that once had covered the entire barnyard. Roses need good drainage.

But I like to think there's another reason they grow so well. About twenty years ago when I was shredding cornstalks the machine jammed. Forgetting that one must always detach the sparkplug wire before cleaning out debris from the sharp blades, I looked down to see a beautiful mound of scarlet and green. The blades had started rotating and had sliced off the middle fingers of my left hand. Well, after getting them sewed up in the emergency room, I took that bloody compost and spread it on the roses. Not many men have recycled themselves to be reincarnated as a rose. Anyway they've bloomed mightily ever since. I picked a perfect red one and took it to my wife's bedstand and grinned remembering the time I put a similar red rose in the toilet bowl before she got up one morning. With the rose still dripping in her hand she came down and kissed me. "Oh Cully," she said, "You're still the crazy nut I married years ago."

The strawberry bed also needed weeding so I went out to begin that task. As I passed my thirty foot compost bed I felt very wealthy. All that careful layering of leaves, grass and horse manure would produce many loads of the crumbly black humus that had made the gardens so productive. Now the garden had been rototilled and seeded with annual rye grass and it was one lush green carpet. Not so my strawberry bed. Lord, there were so many tall weeds I could scarcely see the plants.

Cautioning myself not to overdo, I began the job but didn't quit in time. Suddenly I began to feel dizzy and the next I knew I was lying there with my nose buried in the soil. Was this the next episode of heart failure my doctor had warned me about? No, though the heart was beating rapidly it was not irregular and there was no gasping. I'd just suffered a blackout, a TIA or transient ischemic attack such as I'd often experienced some years ago. As I lay there I recalled the similar one I'd had in the U.P. when blazing a trail around Porcupine Bluff. Nothing to really worry about but I shakily returned to the house.

Why had that blackout happened now after so many years of being free from them? Perhaps it was because I'd been bending over too long as I pulled those weeds. In the past that had often made me dizzy. The thought came to me that perhaps my blood sugar was too low, that I'd had some diabetic hypoglycemia, so I checked my blood sugar level on the glucometer and the reading was only 42, far too low a level. I hadn't had such a level since I gave up shooting myself with insulin. Pulling out of my pocket the little bag of sugar lumps I always carry I chewed down two of them and drank a glass of milk. Soon I was feeling fine. No big deal!

Deciding I'd better take it easy I went to my study for a book to read. As always it was a visual mess. Books line three of the walls and above my typewriter are two short shelves holding the 37 books I've written. Most of them are textbooks but my favorites are the Northwoods Readers that have brought me so many new friends and fan letters.

For casual reading I like to choose a book at random and today I reached for one behind my back sight unseen. From the feel of it I knew immediately that it was Mackenzie's "Five Thousand Receipts: Practical Library". Bound in tattered leather and now held together by a rubber band, it had come from New Jersey to Michigan with my great grandparents before the Civil War by canal boat, sailing schooner and covered wagon.

The book, published in 1829, is a fat one with very fine print. Designed for pioneers, it contains instructions for doing almost everything a settler might need to do in a new land. There are sections on agricultural practices, bees, brewing, engraving, metallurgy, indeed on any subject needed for living or survival. Opening the book I read:

"Utility of sheep dung. This is used in dyeing for the purpose of preparing cotton and linen to receive certain colours, particularly the red, which it performs by impregnating the stuffs with an animal mucilage of which it contains a great quantity."

As I browsed through the book I learned how to shoe an ox, make perfume, force rhubarb, know good mushrooms, manufacture glass and build a barn. A large segment of the book dealt with medicine and this is what it said about my congestive heart failure - then called dropsy of the chest: "Symptoms: Great difficulty breathing especially when lying down, oppression and weight in the chest, countenance pale, pulse irregular, dry cough and violent palpitation." Yes, that was what I had experienced. "Treatment: This is one of the diseases that mock the art of man. To say that it is incurable would be hazarding too much but as yet it has nearly always proved so. All that can be done is to use purging, emetics, diuretics and to have the patient abstain from any heavy toil." Not much medical progress in 170 years.

Because my eyes were tiring from the fine print I looked out of the wavy panes of my study window to see if the mail had come and the red flag on the mailbox showed that it had. Rather than go down the lane I walked along the east lilac hedge that borders the long front lawn picking off the spent flowers of red cannas and yellow marigolds that border it. When those lilacs bloomed next spring, would I be here to see them? Of course I would, and I'd bring great armfuls back to make the house fragrant. Disappointed to find only catalogues and circulars, I was elated when I found a package addressed to Cully Gage that had come from Laurium in the U.P.

House-Front View

Unwrapping it when I returned, I found a note: "Dear Cully Gage: You don't know me but after reading all your books I feel I know you and that you like saffron bread so here's a loaf from our little bakery." Saving the lady's name and address so I could thank her, I ate the end slice even before taking off my jacket. As our Cornish miners used to say, "I dearly love they saffron bread." My wife used to bake it about once a month and my daughter, Cathy, brings me a loaf on my birthday so it was a real treat. It's hard to find saffron Down Below.

Time for my mandatory nap. How could I do that

35

differently? For one thing, I could change the music. No symphonies for me today. At first I considered playing one of the Yoopers cassettes, the one about the second week in deer camp that became a national hit, but rejected the idea. I'd never rest well listening to those crazy buggers. No, I'd get some Jamaican music and sleep in Abraham's bosom.

Abraham's bosom is one of the five bedrooms in this old house, one of four dormer rooms added by Dr. Henwood from whom we purchased the farm. It is named after the Biblical Abraham who lived happily for 175 years or so the Book of Genesis says. It is a comforting room and all who sleep there arise refreshed. I'd never slept in it.

Lying there with the sun streaming in through the casement windows and listening to Belafonte singing "Island in the Sun" I slept deeply but not until some more good memories had run their course.

Probably because of the music, most of them reflected our two holiday visits to Jamaica. Those visits occurred because one afternoon I was about to go fishing when a Cadillac arrived in our barnyard and a distinguished looking gentleman stepped out. "I'm Malcolm Fraser," he announced. "You may recall our correspondence about whether the term stammering should be used instead of stuttering. No, I'm not here to argue further about the matter but to seek your advice about how to spend a lot of money...."

I interrupted the bugger. "Mr. Fraser," I said. "Had I known you were coming I could have set up an appointment but the fishing fever is on me and I'm not interested in anything else."

"But you don't understand, Dr. Van Riper," he replied, stuttering a little as he did so. "I am the co-founder of NAPA and have established a tax exempt foundation dedicated to the relief of stuttering. To keep that tax exemption the Foundation must annually spend a portion of its considerable income. Perhaps we can give your speech clinic a substantial grant. In any event, I need your counsel since you are one of the most esteemed...."

Again I interrupted him. "No, dammit," I said. "I don't want any of your lousy money. I'm going fishing. Good day!"

As I climbed into my truck I saw him walk dejectedly back to the Cadillac and felt ashamed of myself. I've never liked hurting anyone. So I got out and accosted him. "Mr. Fraser," I asked. "Do you know how to row a boat?" When he nodded affirmatively I told him that if he'd go with me to Atwater Pond and row the boat and not say a damned word until I'd caught five fish with my flyrod I'd give him a glass of whiskey and listen to what he had to say.

But what has that to do with Jamaica? Well I told Malcolm that his Foundation should concentrate on producing books and pamphlets on stuttering because of the widespread ignorance about the disorder, that he should hold conferences to which the best brains in the country could be invited to share their expertise and to create the nuclei for the publications. "You'll have to hold these conferences during the Christmas holidays when they could be available and have them in exotic places to attract them. You should pay all expenses and also provide an honorarium so they can bring their wives along." Well, we've held those conferences in Puerto Rico, Florida, the Virgin Islands, Acapulco, the Bahamas, Hawaii and Jamaica. The project proved very successful and his Speech Foundation of America has done a lot of good.

As I lay there in Abraham's Bosom I was remembering the one we held in Montego Bay, Jamaica. Not the morning or afternoon sessions during which we tried to reach agreement on what should go into the proposed book but those wonderful evenings when we got together singing and drinking rum with a native band of musicians and having a high old time.

Neither my wife nor I nor the others had experienced such luxury. We lived in our own beach cottage complete with maid service and fresh flowers and fruit on the table when we awoke. We breakfasted in a patio covered with vines on ogli fruit, papayas, or anything we wished to order. Late in the evening we dined on escargo, oysters Rockefeller, roast pig or whatever with wine. We strolled the wide beaches and went swimming in the warm salt water. Often I asked myself what a bush bum from the U.P. was doing there.

Oh yes, and there was the occasion of Milove's seventieth birthday. I'd forgotten to bring along any present for her and our schedule prevented any shopping so I paid ten dollars to a handsome young beach boy to give her a loud wolf whistle every time he saw her. "She's the old gal in the red and white dotted bikini," I said, "the one with a fine figure."

"I've already noticed her, sir," he replied. "It will be a pleasure." Milady Katy had a fine birthday.

Realizing that for months I'd been lunching on soup, half a sandwich, milk and fruit I decided I'd eat the same things I did when hiking cross country to Lake Superior. I hard boiled an egg, cut off a small chunk of bologna and had some korpua, the delicious hard cinnamon toast of the Finns. I cheated a bit on the tea by not steeping it in a clean sock in the worm can. I ate that lunch under the pines of my park. Very good!

When I reentered the house I found a huge box in the shed. United Parcel Service had brought the bushel of daffodils I'd ordered last spring to naturalize them in the grassy area east of the pool. Well, I couldn't possibly plant them now. Perhaps I could get Ted Redmond, a husky high school kid who lived across the road, to do it for me. But I love to plant promises so much I just had to try. Getting the posthole digger and a pail of compost mixed with bonemeal I began to dig some holes next to the fireplace where the earliest flowers bloom in the spring. I dug just one hole and quit because I knew if I dug more I'd have some trouble. Using a posthole digger is hard work. Fighting off a bit of depression I sat on the bench round the big oak tree and smoked a pipe of Sir Walter Raleigh.

This need to curtail one's activities and to fit them to one's limitations is one of the hardest things an old person has to accept. I've always liked to live recklessly, not carefully. That's why I once hiked cross country all the way from Lake Superior to Tioga in one day, a distance of forty miles. The thought of that trip, however, brought back some fine memories of spring in the U.P. Not of daffodils but of yellow cow slips, the early marsh marigolds. And of the white, blue and yellow violets that were everywhere in the woods, and of the arbutus, pink and white, with its fine fragrance.

On that long hike whole hardwood hillsides were carpeted by spring beauties, the tiny pink striped flowers so thick that I left footprints in them. Patches of trillium proudly wore their three large white petals under their green umbrellas; clumps of Dutchman's breeches were spaced with adder's tongues and blood root; occasionally I found a rare pink lady's slipper. We didn't need daffodils up there in the springtime.

Wanting to do something constructive that wouldn't require a lot of effort I decided to clean the cowbarn. That area is at the east end of the old barn and still contains the stanchions where the cows were milked, not that I've milked any there. As a boy I sometimes had to do the milking when Mrs. Waisenen who usually did it was sick. Old Rosey, our Jersey cow, was a cantankerous beast who liked to kick me off the stool or spill the milk pail. I got no pleasure from interminably squeezing her teats except when directing a stream of the milk into the mouth of a waiting cat. Over the years here I've had horses, pigs and chickens but no cow.

The cowbarn wasn't very dirty except for the droppings under the swallows' nests on the beams above and I had it cleaned up in short order. Then I went into the space behind the stanchions and swept that with the push broom and noticed something covered by a tarp. When I removed the latter I began to laugh until my sides ached. I had uncovered the mynah birds' cage.

All my life I've wanted a parrot I could teach to sing or cuss or stutter but once when I told my wife I was thinking of buying one she vetoed it with such vehemence that I gave up the idea. It seems that when she was a child she'd been bitten by one when she tried to feed it a peanut rather than a cracker.

When I mentioned that to a graduate course in speech development one of my students told me that his uncle, a psychologist at the University of Cincinnati, had just finished an experiment on the social behavior of mynah birds from India, birds that had been reared in complete isolation from each other. He said he might be able to get them for me. I told him to get them if he could because mynah birds can be taught to speak as well as parrots.

I was delighted when he returned from his Christmas vacation with them and, my wife being away at the time, I set up their big cage in my study. A fait accompli! When she returned and found them she was hot tongued for a bit but calmed down when I told her it was only a temporary experiment in teaching birds to talk and that mynahs weren't parrots. I said I'd do all the caretaking and she could keep the study door closed. "OK," she said, "I'll give you a month and then let in the cat."

The psychologist had told my student that trying to teach them to talk was a hopeless task, that their long isolation would make it impossible and that the age of speech readiness had long been passed. In reply, the student had told his uncle that I was the best speech therapist in the world and that I'd prove him wrong.

When I told The Madam that my reputation was at stake, she sniffed, a most unwise thing to do if you have mynah birds in the vicinity. Like geese, they are dirty birds, producing incredible amounts of excrement with a stink that would wither the nostrils of a polecat. Though the mynahs are long gone from my study and many years have passed, I can still smell Jack and Jackie every time it rains.

According to some psychologists, birds learn to talk because the human beings who tend them speak to them as they are being fondled or fed. Then, whenever the bird happens to make a similar sound, it remembers the feeling's of comfort and relief that had been associated with those sounds and so emits more of them to get that rewarding experience. The bird must also fall in love with you or it won't talk. That means you must love it too.

Well, I tried but it's hard to love a dirty bird with a quivering and squirting hind end. Besides, Jack and Jackie were not at all loveable. They regarded me with hostile eyes and tried constantly to take a chunk out of my fingers when I sought to touch them or clean out their cage which needed it hourly. Finally I learned how to slip one newspaper in and the other one out without being pecked to the bone. I had to subscribe to the New York Times to keep even with their south ends. Lord, how they shat!

And they were mute as a stone. Not even a twitter did I hear those first days. Perhaps the psychologist was right. The birds had been reared in separate cages; now they shared one and I hoped that love or lust might give a more favorable prognosis. One trouble was that I wasn't really sure that Jack and Jackie were of different sexes. Perhaps they were mynahsexuals. They did peck at each other perfunctorily but did not ogle or preen. Why was I spoiling my life with feathered imbeciles? But I've had other resistant patients and have taught mute children and deaf ones to talk. There was always a way. All problems had solutions. I changed another newspaper.

The insight finally came. They needed a model with whom they could identify. Having never heard another bird, they had to hear birdsong. Not having any canaries I went to the piano and played "Listen to the Mocking Bird" on the highest notes of the keyboard. Immediately they began to hop around excitedly, ruffling their feathers and cocking their heads to one side. Then, as I continued to play, they began to utter sounds of great variety: gurglings, whistles, rattles, cackles and a few true vowels. I hurriedly fed them and left the study hollering "Eureka!" like Archimedes in his bathtub. The Madam surveyed me coldly. "Happy New Year," she said .

That weekend I hardly left the study except to eat. Once my wife brought me a sandwich, a birdseed sandwich, but I had found a way to get them to vocalize. I could do it every time-just play the black keys on the piano and the birds would stop crapping and start making sounds. All I had to do was to reinforce with food the human sounding vowels that they produced and then later to shape these into human utterance. My first target was to be "Hello!", then later I would teach them to say, "Hello, you damned psychologist," and send them back to him to crap in his lap. Or so I dreamed.

The training was difficult. Once I got them vocalizing to the piano I had to imitate their vowels in unison, then feed them quickly with a few sunflower seeds, their favorite food. Under this schedule the number of their vowel sounds markedly increased. A transcription of one morning's utterances yielded the following: Jack: a (as in cat) 68 times; e (as in met) 6 times; o five times. Jackie said about the same but also combined two vowels to produce a-o and eh-o. These I recorded on a tape recorder and I could identify which one was speaking because Jack's pitch was lower than that of the other mynah. Surprisingly, they rarely spoke at the same time but took turns. So did I.

After about a week of this training, The Madam opened the study door and presented me with a care package. The birds eyed me with interest as I unwrapped it. Inside were pictures of my children and of the university, a jar of peanut butter, some crackers and a safety razor blade with a note saying, "I'm not going home to mother, no matter what!" Somehow I got the impression that she was hinting at something.

I'll have to admit that I was getting pretty sick of those dirty devils by that time. Often I had the disturbing thought that they were training me rather than I training them, making me bring them food and drink and play the piano and clean their damned cage. Often they seemed to smile!

When one day I heard Jack chuckle and Jackie produce a very human sounding laugh, I knew that I needed emancipation so I went down to the university and brought home a new recorder with a voice-activated switch that would turn on automatically whenever the birds made a sound. I then prepared a loop of tape on which I recorded my rendition of Listen to the Mocking Bird and my loving imitations of their vowels, especially the eh-o combinations, and "Hello" spoken in a high falsetto. It worked! Through the closed study door I listened and found that the birds were talking more than when I was in the room. So I kissed Milove and went ice fishing. As I knelt there, slowly congealing, watching the cork in the hole and breathing fresh air for a change, I felt a tingle of triumph. I'd outwit those birdy bastards yet. A man had more brains than a mynah.

After two days of this tape recorder therapy Jack and Jackie were producing the two target vowels profusely and saying them in sequence and even at times saying something that sounded like hello. Then I made a new tape loop that just said the hello over and over again.

Finally one morning when I opened the study door I was greeted by a very clear "Hello" from Jackie. La dee dah! I did The Dance of the Wild Cucumber and called my wife, but the damned bird wouldn't do it again. The Madam gave me one of those strange looks that had characterized her of late, held her nose, and departed without a word.

But Jackie had said hello, and said it a lot of other times that day. I turned on the other recorder and left for the university. When I returned, I played the recording with great anticipation. Yes, I'd done it. Both birds were saying hello although Jack's rendition sounded more like "Allah," A Moslem bird, no doubt, though he didn't say it at all prayerfully. No problem! I could shape his Allah into Hello. I slept well that night, though again alone. How long had it been that Milove had moved to another bedroom?

The next morning I arose before dawn, entered the dark study, changed the newspapers in the cage, filled the pellet container, set the two recorders to going and left for the university, planning to return at 9:30 for a late breakfast. At 8:30 my secretary barged into my office. "Your wife is on the phone and she's crying and swearing and told me to get you even if you're in class. I think you'd better answer it."

The Madam was almost incoherent in her fury but I got the message. I'd left the cage door open when I changed the papers in the dark and left the study door open too. Those damned birds of mine were flying all over the house, defecating everywhere and she had locked herself in the kitchen and couldn't get her coat and hat to get out of there and when I got home and I'd better get home soon, she'd strangle me with her own hands and enjoy every gasp. There was more sobbing and terror and insult. I hung up the receiver and scratched my head. It was more than a crisis; it was a domestic catastrophe. It was a choice between Milove or two dirty birds. She was a fine woman; she had given me three fine children. She had given me love and apple pie.

So I called in the student who had brought me the birds, told him to buy a long handled net and to get the hell out to my house, catch the birds and take them to our biology department if he hoped to have his assistantship renewed. And then to go back and clean up the mess.

When I got home at noon the birds were gone and with the exception of a broken lamp and two shattered pictures all was well. For half an hour she gave me the silent treatment and then let me have it. I hunched my head down into my neck and bore it, feeling like the peasant described by the Roman poet Horace who waited for the river to run by so he could cross. Once again I was glad I'd had a classical education because I recalled the tale of Socrates who, staggering home one night after some boozy dialogues with the boys, had found the door locked. When he knocked, his wife opened the window above the door and laced into him. Like my wife, Xantippe was most eloquent when furious, and like Milove, the longer she ranted the madder she got. Finally she even got a chamber pot and dumped its contents onto the head of the philosopher. Socrates stood there and wiped his brow. "After the thunder, comes the rain," said he.

All things, good and evil, eventually end. The Madam forgave me and we lived many years in domestic tranquility ever since. Except once, when on a damp day she entered my study and I said "Ello!, Ello," in a high falsetto.

The rest of this day passed quietly but always differently. For Happy Hour I drank wine instead of scotch, ate my supper standing up, and went to bed, climbing the back stairs instead of the front ones. It had been another good day.

DAY THREE

This day began at two in the morning in the middle of the Manistee National Forest in southern Michigan when John Eaton and his akita dog went outdoors to relieve themselves.

But I'd better make some introductions. John Eaton came to do part time work for me shortly after my wife died six years ago. After serving four years in the Marine Corps he decided to get a college education and needed to work to supplement the meager college subsidy given to four year veterans. A short but very tough and strong man and very intelligent, he has become a fine companion, friend, almost a son. He mows my lawns, does my banking, dresses my surgical wounds, buys my groceries, rototills the gardens, and with the chainsaw has kept my barn filled with wood for the winters. Indeed, he does everything I used to do but cannot do now. I've often taken him up to my lakes deer hunting and fishing and he loves that land almost as much as I do. I've been blessed and very lucky to have found him.

The akita is John's dog of a hunting breed that served Japanese royalty for centuries. Bigger than a German shepherd, it is covered with a heavy white coat of hair except for a black face and pointed ears that stick straight up. John calls him Teddy which doesn't fit his dignity at all. He should be called Hirohito or something such. Usually very aloof, Teddy likes me and we howl at each other whenever we meet. Hunting the farm joyously, he has killed many of the woodchucks that have plagued me for years. I've always had dogs, mostly springer spaniels, but for obvious reasons do not have one now. Perhaps that is why I enjoy Teddy so much.

What were we doing up there in my little cabin on Gut Lake? I guess it was that my hunger to see the fall colors had overcome my good sense. This year many of my U.P. correspondents had written that the foliage was absolutely spectacular, the best it had ever been and they had pictures to prove it. Photos, however, are no substitute for the real thing. For many years I've made the long trip north to see them and, before the heart failure, had intended to do so again. Down here the autumn colors are dull, mainly dirty yellows or the bronze of oak, None of the little sugar maples I'd brought down had survived to burst into red flame as they do in the U.P. Why are the fall colors so much better up north? Perhaps the Lord thoroughly soaks the souls up there with gorgeous colors so they can make it through the long months of black and white.

Feeling that I needed some of that soaking if I too were to survive the winter I decided to spend the weekend at the little cabin because it is only about a three hour drive from here and because in other years I've found some fairly good colors there around our little lake. Knowing my doctor would probably say no, I didn't tell him. So one Friday evening after John had finished his work on the construction job, north we went.

Before we started I told John we'd make two stops, first at the rest stop on US-131 near Grand Rapids and the other at Half Moon Lake Park near the little town of Grant. I'd get out, walk around, and then decide whether to continue or to return. Even though the colors along the roadside were no better than those here, it was good to be heading north.

When we reached the rest area I was feeling fine and told John to drive on but by the time we reached Half Moon Lake the usual profound fatigue was present though my pulse was strong and regular. Teddy loves that park and knows every tree in it so we spent fifteen minutes there as I recuperated. By this time it was dusk and on we went through Grant, Newago and White Cloud. Crossing the Muskegon River at Newago I told John how once a friend and I had canoed down to that bridge from the headwaters, a two and a half day trip. Sure couldn't do it now. Finally, just south of Baldwin, we left M-37 and took a road to Bitely, then westward to the little dirt road that goes to our cabin in the forest, seeing in the headlights one deer and the eyes of several others.

While John took off the padlocks, removed the internal shutters from the windows and made a fire, I sat in the car before staggering in to flop myself down in the big Morris chair. I felt triumphant. Damned if I hadn't made it. While Teddy roamed in the dark woods, John fixed me a good dollop of whiskey and water which made me feel even better. Hell, I'd be able to make it back to the U.P. next spring. The exhilaration didn't last long, however, and after a sandwich and some milk I crawled into my sleeping bag and fell asleep instantly.

It must have been John banging the gong that woke me. Oh yes, I should tell you about that gong. It's really a large brass cymbal, the kind they use in a band or orchestra. It hangs about four feet from the ground from a cross bar between two trees right in front of the cabin. Camp Rule No.1 states that any man who has to take a leak must do so under the gong, then celebrate his masculinity by banging it with his dong while yelling "Ow!" So far as I know, no one has ever obeyed that rule due to shortage of courage, stature, or appendage and a convenient club also hangs from the crossbar so they can pretend to have done so.

Anyway, the gong woke me but soon I was asleep again.

Shortly thereafter John was tugging at my sleeping bag. "I need some help," he said."Teddy has tangled with a porcupine. Having once stepped on some quills, I put on my shoes to see Teddy's face covered with them.We tried rolling him in a blanket and pulling out the quills with pliers but there were just too many of them. All of us had a hard night and I slept little because Teddy kept trying to crawl in with me for comfort. Finally came the dawn and after a short breakfast I told John to take Teddy to Baldwin in search of a veterinarian, and if there were none in that town, to any other place where he might find one, even if it meant going back to Grand Rapids.

They didn't return until afternoon but a vet in Reed City had done a fine job. John said he had to remove over fifty quills while the dog was sedated.

So I had the morning to myself and it was a very good one. Venturing outside I found our little lake surrounded with scarlet and clear yellow contrasts with the green of the pines I'd planted years ago. I sat on a log for a long time just looking.

Then, needing to limber up the old legs I walked the trails, finding memories with every step.The rhododendrons I had planted were eight feet tall, the three mountain ash had berries and robins in them; the dogwoods wore that indescribable pink sheen. As far as I could see, the open woods were dotted with pines and spruce that had been only six inch seedlings when I planted them. When we first built the cabin twenty six years ago there had been no green firs at all, just poplars, soft maples and oaks. A man from the U.P. needs firs and pines in his forest so I had put in over four thousand of them. They are my children too. When a bright yellow leaf zigzagged down and settled on my head I wore it back to the cabin. I had been anointed.

Opening the cabin door I noticed that above the doorway the phoebes had left the nest they had built there year after year. How they would scold us with their name when we opened it! I also recalled the sound of whippoorwills and the gobbles of wild turkeys. Once again the magic of the forest was healing me and making me young again.

This was Milove's favorite cabin though she loved those in the U.P. too, especially the old hunting cabin where we'd honeymooned. Perhaps it was that here the forest was not so wild or threatening. Besides she had selected the site, and bought all the furnishings. Here she roamed freely without having to watch out for bears. She never forgot the time when we were trout fishing on the Tioga and a mother bear chased us away from her cub and we got back to the car just before the bear did.

How vividly I felt her presence! There on the far wall hung her red rain jacket, her sweater, and the silly little hat she'd purchased in the Bahamas. On a sunny afternoon she'd row out into the middle of Gut Lake (which she insisted was Blue Lake), lie down in the bottom and let the boat drift with the wind.

Even the log walls reminded me of her. Because of the many coats of preservative she'd put on them they seemed almost newly cut while outside they had turned grey. I found the camp log in which both of us had written much about the doings of our days there and opened it to see her handwriting. "September 7-9. Cully and I got here after dark again in the rain and someone had burned up all the firewood I'd sawed after lugging maple poles from the lakeshore. Don't you ever do that again without replacing them." "June 17, 1972. Cully was napping when I looked out the window to see four wild turkeys striding up the road, one a very big one with a wide fan tail and red wattles below its beak but by the time I roused him they were gone. He saw their big forked tracks though so he knew I hadn't been imagining."

Yet another item from the log: "I am blessed to be back here with the man I love. He had the coffee made and the pancakes too before he tickled my feet to wake me up. Luxury!"

Still feeling the effects of the trip and loss of sleep, I crawled into the bunk again and didn't awaken until John and Teddy returned. The akita seemed to be in fine shape and after a swift lunch they left to do some flyfishing though I told John it would probably be fruitless. There were no flies and at that time of the year the bass and bluegills would be deep. They went anyway though Teddy wouldn't enter the boat but just prowled the shoreline, then swam out to the boat and almost tipped it over when John hauled him into it. That ended the fishing. As they climbed the steep hill from the lake I envied them knowing I'd never be able to do that again. Yet it was very good just to be sitting on the steps surrounded by beauty.

Just west of Gut Lake lies another little lake, Bass Lake, a shallow one surrounded by muskeg. I think I told about it once in one of my Northwoods Readers because I almost drowned in it. I'd shot a goose and trying to reach it with a long pole by going out on that floating muskeg I almost drowned but I had survived. I would survive this heart trouble too. Along the northwest shore of Bass Lake there often are cranberries in the muskeg moss and for years my wife and I had gathered our Thanksgiving cranberries there so I asked John to see if he couldn't find some. To show him the old logging road that went to the lake I walked

47

part way with him and the akita and was bushed when I returned. It's hard to grow old. Taking a folding camp chair I brought it out to the firepit where we do most of our summer cooking. A little breeze had sprung up and the tall poplars waved their tall tops slowly back and forth shedding a few yellow leaves with each swing. As I sat there I remembered how Ken Frielink and I had tried to dig a well there. One of the few bad features of this little cabin is that we have to bring up our drinking water in jugs because the lake water is too full of sediment except for use in cooking.

When I was a boy in the U.P. there was an old man named Nels Peterson who was the town's dowser. Everyone said that he could always find good water and called on him before they dug their open wells. The story was that a man who thought dowsing was all nonsense once dug a hole five feet down and planted a jug of water in it, then after the field had been plowed and planted to oats, he challenged Nels to find the jug. It took Nels only ten minutes to find it or so the tale went. I, myself, watched the old man picking a well site for the Plankeys who lived three doors down from us. With a forked branch that had a substantial stub, Nels curled his fingers over each branch, held it horizontally before him and walked around the yard. Suddenly the stub went down as though some hidden force had hold of it. I could see the tension in his arms as he resisted the pull. "Dig yer well here," he told the Plankeys and when they did they found fine water only nine feet down. Nels said that the best dowsing sticks came from willow or applewood but that many people didn't have the feel for deep water that he did. He also said he had so much of it he'd even found water with a wire coat hanger.

Ken borrowed a drilling rig from a friend and we loaded it onto my truck with four sections of pipe, a perforated well point and some big monkey wrenches. I brought along a dowsing stick I'd cut from our apple orchard and when we got to the cabin we took turns exploring the area on top of the hill. There was only one spot where the stick dipped a little and that was near the gong so we tried there.

Phew! That drilling was hard work. The drilling rig looked like a guillotine except that instead of a sharp blade there was a very heavy steel bar that slid up and down in the tower's grooves. We first had to crank up the bar so it was above the pipe bearing the drill bit, lock it in place, disengage the chain, then unlock the catch and bam! down it went. Sometimes the blow would pound the pipe down a foot; at other times only a few inches. When the first pipe had been driven, we pulled it up and examined the point. It was dry as a bone with not a hint of water on it. So we added another length of pipe, drove that down too. Nothing! Before giving up we had gone down twenty five feet without finding water. So we drank the rest of the beer, had supper, and went to bed exhausted.

The next morning I was ready to call it quits but Ken suggested that we move the rig down near the lake. "We'll drive down just one length of pipe," he said. "We're bound to find water so close to the lake. Even if it's lake water, it will be filtered enough for drinking."

He was wrong. After all that tough work of dragging the rig down the hill, we again got only a dry hole. Incredible! Why, we'd drilled it not six feet from the water's edge.

I found out later that our lake was what was called a pot hole or fault lake, that when the glacier retreated a great mountain of ice had broken off and settled there compressing the clay beneath it into an impermeable basin.So that is why we bring up our water in jugs.

John and the akita had returned. The dog had chased a raccoon up into a hollow tree and John had found a big handful of cranberries. Remembering The Madam's admonition in the log book and because it was getting much cooler I asked him to get some dry maple poles and cut them with the chainsaw into stove lengths and also to saw and split that big oak limb by the outhouse so we could have good coals for our steaks.

While he did so I took another little walk down the road and on my return I noticed a large oval patch of moss near where we park our car. I blew Milove a kiss. That moss was all that remained of the nine by twelve braided rug that she had made for our living room floor. How hard she had worked on that rug all one winter, cutting and sewing strips, winding them into balls,then doing the hard work of braiding them together. Once I caught her weeping because of the bursitis it gave her but when the rug was finished it was beautiful. Mainly blue and tan, it contained rags made of wool clothing, some of it donated by friends who used to enjoy coming out to identify their old coats and pants. After many years of having dogs and children romping on it or lying on it to watch the fire, the rug began to disintegrate a little. I couldn't bear to throw it away so brought it up to the little cabin for several more years. Finally, when she suggested I take it to the Bitely dump, I spread it out by our parking spot. Now it was moss, beautiful moss. Perhaps I would be moss too someday.

I sat outside for a time by the firepit watching the fire burn down into coals until the trees lost their color, then went inside to build a fire in the stove, light the kerosene lamps and candles, and set the table. Very snug and cozy as always, the radiating warmth felt good. Old bones appreciate warmth and young ones do too on a cool evening.

How beautiful Milove always looked by candlelight, even when she was in her seventies.

The steaks and mashed potatoes were excellent. "Pierre," I said. "You have acquired merit." Full fed, I dozed in my chair while John did the dishes and Teddy munched the steak bones. Then, when John announced that he and Teddy were going for their evening walk by flashlight, I crawled into my sleeping bag and never heard them return.

The next morning I roused when I smelled the coffee and bacon and heard John cooking. He'd made cranberry pancakes, the first I'd ever eaten. They were delicious. Outside it was raining hard so we packed, cleaned up the place, and left for home.

The miles sped by swiftly after I got John to telling about his boot camp experiences in the Marines. He described the "Slide for Life" where he had to climb sixty feet to a platform, then slide down a plastic coated wire over water while the damned drill sergeant tried to shake him off. He told how in the gas chamber he had to take off the gas mask, give his name, rank and serial number, and put the gas mask on again before he could open the door. He described the Stairway to Heaven which consisted of two tall telephone poles with cross pieces increasing spaced so that for the last one he had to jump to reach it. Oh, he had a lot of good tales.

John even began to sing some Marine songs, one of them which went: "I put my hand upon her toe/Yo ho, Yo Ho/ I put my hand upon her toe/ She said, Marine, you're mighty slow/ Yo Ho, Yo ho." The rest of it is unprintable. Then, when we passed through Newago I saw a handprinted sign in a store window advertising an auction bake social. That reminded me of a similar social in Tioga seventy years ago so I told it to John. Here is the tale:

In the Upper Peninsula of Michigan, the U.P., February was the cruelest month of the year. Great drifts of snow confined our people to their homes and each week brought a new blizzard. Spring was just an impossible dream.

However, there was one year when I was a senior in high school that the Methodist church decided to ease our depression by holding an auction box social in the town hall. Hand printed notices were put up in the postoffice and stores: "Free admittance! Dancing! Ice Cream! Auction of baked goods made by pretty girls! Nuts to winter!"

The preparations for the event took a lot of work. Girls and women baked cakes and cookies and pies and put them in gaily decorated boxes. The Town Hall's two big pot bellied stoves had to be fired up for two days and nights. Because my mother had volunteered my services in setting up the tables and chairs and streamers, I was there when the girls brought in their boxes to be placed on the long auction table. I especially noticed the one brought in by Amy Erickson, the prettiest girl in Tioga, thinking I might bid on it myself. No, she was Mullu's girl and I was his friend. I'd tell him that her box was the one with the yellow and red ribbons. There was one other box, the biggest one, almost two feet square and bearing an artificial rose on its top. When Billy Simons, our Sunday School Superintendent, saw who brought it I was shocked to hear that pious man swear for five minutes. Aunt Lizzie had brought it. 'Oh, that damned old fool," he roared. "She'll put the kibosh on the bidding, she will that!" Aunt Lizzie had buried three husbands but she was still looking, and still thought of herself as a girl though she was in her late sixties.

By suppertime everything was ready. Twenty chairs were set along the west wall where the girls who brought boxes would sit; three more by one stove for the accordion players, and the table for the cookie and ice cream server was by the other. A big blue enamel coffee pot was kept warm on that one too.

Near the stage was the auctioneer's table and change box. Behind the stage were bleachers for those who didn't want to bid but wanted to see the fun.

We usually eat supper early in winter time so the doors opened at seven and soon quite a crowd had assembled. Most of them just bought an ice cream cone and cookie and sat in the bleachers to watch the doings. Then the girls filed in to sit on the chairs and among them was Aunt Lizzie wearing one of her wedding dresses and with a little blue bow in her wig. Then men and boys went over to the auction table to examine the boxes, shaking and sniffing, before forming a cluster by a stove to wait for the auction to begin.

Billy Simons, the auctioneer, laid down the rules. The first bid must be at least twenty five cents and increments of no less than ten cents would be allowed. The men should step forward before bidding to identify themselves. When he banged his gavel, the bidding was over and the last bidder got the box. He would then open the box and show its contents to everyone before picking up the card that said, "Congratulations. Your partner for the evening is so and so. Take the box to her and then dance. After the auction is over there will be free dancing for everyone."

Although I had no intention of bidding I was there with my

friends Mullu and Fisheye among the men when I had a brilliant idea. I'd tell Mullu, who was nuts about Amy, which box was hers but I'd tell Toivo Maki who had bullied us for years and who also had a crush on Amy that Aunt Lizzie's big box was really Amy's. A dirty trick but I had a lot to get even for. Wait a minute! I'd better not tell Toivo that or he'd kill me! So I called Mullu and Fisheye aside and told them my plan. We'd go over by Toivo and let him overhear me telling Mullu that the big box was Amy's, and Mullu should make the first bid on it. Then he should drop out after Toivo started bidding and Mullu could really bid on the real box of Amy's which I described. Mullu protested at first. "But what if Toivo doesn't fall for it?" he asked,"and I'm stuck with Aunt Lizzie? Hell, they'll laugh me out of town." We assured him that someone was sure to bid for that big box so he agreed. And the deed was almost done.

After the band played its first number the auction began and at first it looked as though it would be a disaster. When Billy picked up the first box at random and held it in the air nobody bid. Nobody! He picked up another and the silence was deafening. We knew why. All the men were looking at Aunt Lizzie and anticipating the outrageous kidding they'd suffer for months if the box they got was Aunt Lizzie's.They weren't playing any Russian roulette, no sir!

Finally when Billy held up a third box Pipu Verlaine bid fifty cents because Marie, his girl friend, had tipped him off. That broke the ice somewhat. A few other men upped the bid and it finally sold for Pipu's ninety cents. Another box brought a dollar from Eino Hyry who showed all of us the delectable angel food cake before taking it to Lempi Salo, his long time girl friend. The band played a waltz and Pipu and Eino and their girls danced. After two more boxes went without any bids, Billy Simons got mad and gave the men hell. He shamed them; he cajoled them; he reminded them how hard so many pretty girls had worked. Then he held up the big box. "Now which of you boogers has the guts to bid a quarter for this lovely one. In it must be a big cake, and cookies, even a pie? Who'll pay a lousy quarter for all this and a pretty girl too?"

Mullu gulped his bid of fifty cents and Toivo countered with seventy five. Other men joined in. Great excitement! Even when the bidding hit a dollar, Toivo wouldn't give in."One fifty!" yelled another man and you could see Toivo sweating. When you earned only five cents for felling and limbing a big spruce tree, that was big money, but when Amy smiled at him, up he went. Finally, at two fifty the auctioneer yelled sold and banged his gavel. Toivo forked over the money to Billy and opened the box.

Yes, there was a huge chocolate cake inside and some peanut butter cookies and other stuff too. The crowd ooh'd and ah'd. "Who's yer partner, Toivo?" they yelled.

Toivo reached for the card and stood there stunned, then bolted from the hall with Aunt Lizzie after him though not before she'd snatched up her box. "Bet she catches him," one man yelled. "Naw, Toivo can run like a deer," shouted another.

After things quieted down, the auction went very well and all of the boxes were sold and lots of people had a high old time doing the polka for the rest of the evening. The church gained over fifty dollars and Tioga had a break in the middle of winter.

We got back to the farm and after a bite to eat I slept until evening. It had been a fine weekend and I hadn't had a bit of heart trouble. I'd be back, Old Cabin.

DAY FOUR

As I opened the back door and saluted the new morning I saw that it would be another fine Indian summer day, most surprising because November rarely had them. We'd had two light frosts, enough to wither most of the flowers, though some of the more sheltered ones were still blooming, but very low temperatures had been predicted and probably would soon be forthcoming. I decided to have breakfast in my Secret Garden.

I wish you could see that Secret Garden in all of its spring or summer glory although even now just before winter begins it is still a beautiful spot. Located against the west wall of the garage and encircled by dense flowering shrubs and a fence covered with vines, visitors would never know it was there unless I showed them.

Secret Garden

In its center stands a crabapple tree and about it are circles of red and white impatiens, begonias and red salvias creating one huge bouquet. These in turn are surrounded by a circular path and outside it grow lilies, cardinal flowers, astilbe and many annuals. Springtime brings a riot of crocus, daffodils and tulips. Now, in November just the flowers around the crabapple tree were still blooming.

I had my breakfast, a modest one, sitting within an arbor covered by clematis and wild cucumber vines. Across from me a fountain leaped in a large cast iron kettle once used for scalding hogs in the fall or for boiling down maple syrup in the spring. Watching that fountain flinging its droplets about in wild abandon almost hypnotizes me. For both Milove and me the Secret Garden has been a sanctuary within a sanctuary.

It certainly wasn't a very beautiful area when we bought the farm in 1945 but just a garbage dump full of junk. rusty cans, and broken bottles. For a few years after I cleaned it out we used the space as a chicken yard with the coop being in the north section of the garage. Behind the arbor where we sit is a hole in the garage covered by a plaque which reads: "And they shall sit, every man under his own vine and under his fig tree: Micah 4:4". Through that hole the chickens entered their yard until the foxes entered it too and made way with them. Though I still sit under the vine our hard winters made it necessary to bring the fig tree into the house where it has flourished for decades, yielding just one fig in all that time and that was inedible.

The breakfast I brought out to the arbor was a sparse one, just an orange, two pieces of toast and a chunk of Havarti cheese. I guess I was just too anxious to get out into the Secret Garden . But as I ate it I tried to recall the best breakfasts I'd ever had. Two of them came to mind immediately, the first one in a quaint little hotel in Ireland and the other on top of Donegal's Bluff in the U.P.

Having had an Irish ancestress, my wife had always wanted to go to Ireland so when Dr.Damste of the University of Utrecht in The Netherlands asked me to come there to help dedicate his new speech clinic I told her she could have two weeks in the Emerald Isle. Once there, we hired a driver, Malachi McMullen, to help us explore the back roads in the southeast corner of the country along the River Shannon and the coast. It was a wonderful trip. I caught some trout in a lake below an old castle; we had tea beside a peat fire in an ancient stone cottage; we met a caravan of gypsies on a little winding road lined with great mossy stones. And we had that breakfast.

It wasn't anything fancy, just oranges, coffee, scones with marmalade and an omelet. But what an omelet! Milove always was proud of her omelets with good reason. She baked them in the oven and insisted we eat them immediately before they fell because they were two inches tall.

But the one we had in Killarney , a ham omelet, surpassed even the best ones of Milove. Fully three inches tall and with a light brown crust, it so impressed my wife that she went to the kitchen to ask the chef how he'd made it. "My husband says I make the best omelet in America," she told the little red haired cook, "but yours is much better. Please tell me your secret."

He grinned. "Ah, ma'am," he replied. "'Tis no secret. I just use a bicycle pump to aerate the whipped eggs." When we got home and I offered to buy her a bicycle pump she said no, that from his grin she knew he'd just been kidding.

The only other breakfast that could compare with that Irish one I ate on top of Donegal's Bluff which is the first one north of the fourth bridge on the Huron Bay Grade road near Tioga. That very tall bluff rising alone from the plain was named after Old Blue Balls, Tioga's tough school superintendent, because he had tented on top of it for a week in June one year when the mosquitoes and black flies were so fierce camping down on the river bank was not bearable. I was there to escape them too.

Arising at dawn from the balsam bed I'd made the evening before I cooked coffee and six small brook trout, frying them with bacon until they were almost crisp, then eating them as I would sweet corn. These with korpua and a pint of wild strawberries comprised that wonderful breakfast. Perhaps it was my surroundings that made the meal so memorable. High up on that great granite hill I could see the Tioga winding for a mile or more, a curving ribbon of white fog tinted a delicate pink by a rising sun.

There in the Secret Garden as I was smoking my pipe after a lesser breakfast John Eaton and his akita dog, Teddy,appeared. As he always does, the dog ran right to the fountain to drink from it as John said, "Don't you think we'd better get rid of some of these early fallen leaves?"

I told him to do so but to shred them first with the big tractor and to put them in the old horse drinking trough or the holding cage by the compost heap. As he left to get the tractor I envied him. I've always loved putting the farm to bed for the winter, always enjoyed playing in the leaves. While doing the breakfast dishes and tidying up the house I thought about how we got ready for winter in the U.P. When leaves had fallen a flurry of activity spread all over Tioga. The chicken coop behind my father's hospital had to be filled a foot deep with leaves, the old sawdust from the ice house shoveled out to make room for the new ice we'd get from the lake, the collapsible storm shed for the front door had to be reassembled. Inside our house the big radiant coal stove with its isinglass windows had to be brought from the woodshed into the living room by Charlie Olafson, the only man in town strong enough to handle it. Stove pipes were taken down and cleaned and chains lowered down the chimneys to scrape off the creosote. All the house windows were washed before putting on the storm windows.

Our clotheslines were full of woolen clothing and my father's beaverskin coat and hat to eliminate the smell of moth balls. Dad's 1914 Model-T Ford needed to be jacked up and put on blocks. Not until after the spring break-up made the two-rut roads passable again would it be used.

One of my jobs was to sandpaper the runners of the cutter (sleigh) until they gleamed because it was in it that my father made his house calls. I also rubbed neatsfoot oil on all the harness of Old Billy, the horse that pulled the cutter. Also, since he often made calls on snowshoes I revarnished the webbing.

At this time of year it was always fun to go down into our cellar. From long hanging shelves, filled with jars of fruit and jellies, hung cabbages, braided onions and the like. In one corner sat a big barrel of apples; in another were crocks of sauerkraut or pickles. Three large bags of potatoes lay against one wall, a crate of rutabagas near them. On the dirt floor mouse traps and rat traps held their cheeses. We were ready for winter. Let it come!

Hearing John on the big tractor I just couldn't stay inside on such a fine day so I began to rake the leaves from the flower beds by the house out onto the lawn so he could shred them. It went very well at first but when I got under the big black walnut tree the leaves were hard to handle because too many twigs clogged the rake. That tree, by the way, is the largest black walnut I've ever seen. It towers above the house and has a circumference of eleven feet. A man once offered me a thousand dollars for it but no deal! Anyway it produces a lot of leaves as well as bushels of nuts, so many I burn them in the fireplace. When I became aware that I was getting out of breath I quit immediately.

As I entered the house the phone rang. After introducing herself, a woman said that she was a newly appointed board member of the Portage Historical Commission and would appreciate being able to tour the old house and hear something of its history. Some of the other members of the board would like to come too. I told her I could see them any time after three that afternoon.

After the phone call I went through the house trying to see it through their eyes. It was clean enough and all I had to do was put away some clothes lying on chairs in my bedroom and to carry some empty fruit jars to the cellar. I've improved a lot in neatness since my wife died, not wanting to become a dirty old man. I do my dishes after each meal and make my bed when I leave it.

Old House - Rear View

The rest of the morning was spent writing my first Christmas cards because I felt I'd better get an early start on them lest my condition deteriorated. Once again I missed Milove who always did that job. After my daily nap and lunch I got the mail and was sitting on the circular bench when my visitors arrived. Strangers sometimes gasp when they enter the house because it is not only very old but very beautiful. These ladies did too. They marveled at the nine foot doors and eleven foot walls and the spaciousness. When I told them the inner walls were also of double brick, they then thumped them to make sure. They noticed the wavy window panes and the heavy white woodwork.

"Please tell us what you know about the history of this lovely old house," they begged.

"Oh, there's too much to tell," I answered. "You can find most of what I know in a book I wrote called 'Our House' which is in the Portage Library. But briefly, it was built before the Civil War in 1859 by Steven Howard who was one of our first settlers to come to this region. Led by his father John Howard who had hauled cannonballs to George Washington's army and who had witnessed the surrender of Cornwallis, the Howards came here in 1831 to build the first log cabin on Dry Prairie across the street from this house. Old John lived long enough to have been in this house many times and to sit by a fire similar to the one you're watching now. In the early years the house was heated by three fireplaces and a cookstove. The one in the dining room has been covered with plaster and wallpaper but you can see the one in my study hidden behind my desk."

When I led them to it they exclaimed over the stuff that clutters my study, the arrowheads I found on the farm, the case of stuffed birds which includes a passenger pigeon shot by my grandmother. The species died out in 1913 so it's a rare item.

One of the women noticed the four foot slab above my desk bearing my carved signature:"Cully Gage" so I had to tell them about my alter ego and show them the Northwoods Readers I'd written under that pen name. I have a set of them with the many textbooks I've written on the double shelf above my typewriter so they soon were exploring. One lady pulled down a copy of the Korean translation of one of them and asked if any of my books had been published in other languages. Questions like that always bug me but I managed to say a polite yes without elaborating.

When they returned to the living room I asked them if they'd like some coffee or tea and when they said they'd prefer the latter I told them they'd have to make it but could use the fragile fluted china cups that had come to Michigan by canal boat, sailing schooner and covered wagon. As they busied themselves in the kitchen I rested in my big armchair and smoked a pipe. I was tiring.

As they sat in the living room sipping their tea and eating the korpua I gave them, I told them some more about the first brick house in Portage. The Howards had held parties here to buy uniforms for the soldiers during the Civil War, according to Steven's granddaughter whom we had interviewed at the age of ninety three when she was in a nursing home. Steven was a short, jolly man with a useless right arm caused when on a very windy day he had gone to the loft of the barn to close the upper door. A strong gust had blown open that door carrying Steven with it and he'd fallen twenty feet to the ground, Despite that bad arm I discovered in the Agricultural Reports for 1870 that he had nine horses, seven pigs, four cows and two hundred sheep; that the farm had produced 700 bushels of corn, 300 bushels of wheat, 400 bushels of oats, thirty tons of hay and six hundred pounds of wool. Not bad for a man with only one good arm. I suppose he had hired help. After Steven and his wife Catharine died, his two sons worked the farm but did not live here. His daughter, Amanda, and her aunt Belda did and when Belda died, Amanda lived here alone until she went insane, tearing off her clothes and dancing nakedly in the fields before they put her in the State Hospital. Sometimes at night I hear her screaming.

The next people to live in the house were the Henwoods.

Dr. Henwood, a highly respected physician, ran a dairy farm here and made numerous improvements to the house including a sunporch and four dormer rooms above its west wing. He also installed a steam furnace and radiators and modernized all the wiring. Dr. Henwood used my study as his dispensary and office. On a warm rainy evening I can smell some of his medicines. After he retired, Dr. Henwood and his wife ran the dairy farm with their son Jim before moving to Florida and selling the house to us. It was Jim Henwood who had planted the two rows of lilacs on each side of our long front lawn. Full of Ho Hum, I suggested that the women might like to see the upstairs."There are five bedrooms and a bath and a sewing room up there," I told them. "You'll find some interesting old furniture and a picture of the house taken shortly after it was built. Take your time and when you come down the back stairs I'll show you the basement."

They were gone a long time for which I was grateful and when they came down I showed them the basement with its hand hewn beams and fieldstone foundation walls. As they passed the big white door to the furnace room they giggled to see the names of my grandchildren scrawled on it. Finally, I took them into the fruit cellar with its shelves full of the wine I'd made long ago and the fruit Milove had canned. I gave each of them a dusty bottle hoping that it had not turned to vinegar. Having learned to drink whiskey, I hadn't opened a bottle of that wine for thirty years.

Before we left the fruit cellar when I asked one of the women to open the cupboard she let out a shriek. "All old houses should have a skeleton in a closet," I said, "and this skull is one I found when I was a youth in the U.P."

"If you'll look closely you'll see that the person was probably killed by a hard blow to the side of the head or perhaps by a mastoid infection. See the hole behind the ear?" Well, that was enough and they soon left. I bet they gobbled all the way home.

As for me, it was Happy Hour and I had another imaginary conversation with Milove who gave me the devil for letting those women see her upstairs. "Oh Cully, don't do that again. It's like showing strangers your underpants. I hope they didn't see my sewing room."

Supper consisted of beef hash from the freezer and a salad because I was too tired to cook a real meal. I did light a candle to make amends to Milove. The two of us always had our evening meal by candlelight.

After supper I put Haydn's Fourth Symphony on the stereo and opened the day's mail, There were a lot of good letters. Here's an excerpt from one of them:

"We lived through a tornado on Palm Sunday in 1965 which took the roof of the house right off us while we were in the basement. We lost all our buildings, barn and all. What a hell of a mess! I don't know if fire is any worse but I sure hope I never have to go through another tornado.

"Tornados do some very strange things - almost beyond the imagination. The wind drove straws into a maple tree next to where our barn was. They were sticking out of that tree as though it were a straw bush and we have pictures to prove it. I had a white straw cowboy hat sitting on the TV next to the west wall of our house. When we came up out of the basement after the storm our house was in bad shape, half on and half off the foundation and both ends were gone. The TV was now in the kitchen area at the opposite end of the house, yet that hat was still on the TV and looked as if it hadn't been moved at all.

"I had bought a set of steel doors, big doors, twelve feet high and ten feet wide, so heavy it took four strong men to lift them and they were blown away so far we never found them. Yet I had a large oval glass picture of my great great grandparents stored in our grainary. After the storm, the building was all gone. The tornado just picked it up and took it away. Nothing was left of it except for the floor and that picture, and the glass on the picture wasn't even broken.

It also blew the feathers off a half dozen chickens we had, some more bare than others. One was a little bantam rooster who was completely naked, Well, come fall, he hadn't grown back any feathers. My wife was feeling sorry for him so she made a pair of little bib overalls and put him in them. Sure looked comical in those britches. One day soon after she made them, a salesman stopped at the house and when he saw him said, '"That's the funniest thing I ever seen.' 'You think that's funny?' said my wife. "You should see him catch one of the hens, hold her down with one claw and try to get those suspenders down with the other.'"

It was time for bed and I climbed the steps without having to pause for rest. Once again I'd had a good day.

DAY FIVE

About three in the morning I awoke from a dream in which I was crossing a turbulent stream on a springy birch log while burdened by a heavy pack sack. It was a precarious business and I was relieved to find myself safe in bed. Not too safe at that because my heart was acting up again. I suppose it was one of those sleep protective dreams such as the one, when the alarm clock is ringing, that you dream you are hearing church bells which means it's Sunday and you don't have to go to work and can continue sleeping. But I couldn't go back to sleep. The irregularity prevented my doing so and I went downstairs to sit in my big chair by a fire still blazing. Sitting up often seems to stabilize the pulse and I took a nitroglycerin pill to help calm it. After some time the heart had slowed down but I slept the rest of the night on the davenport rather than climb the stairs, an act that might have set the heart going haywire again. When again I woke I was feeling fine.

While making my breakfast I thought of the worst cup of coffee I'd ever had. It was in a hotel in Sydney, Australia. Weak, stale, cold and insipid, it was no way to start what was to be a tough day.

I should explain why I was there so far away from home. It happened because of a decision I'd made in 1932 when at last I had conquered my stuttering sufficiently to be able to speak fluently. I decided to plan the rest of my life. I would dedicate my thirties to exploring all the things I'd missed, my forties to creativity, my fifties to becoming wise, my sixties to folly and the rest of my existence to resignation.

I'd followed that plan pretty consistently, getting married and having my first child during my thirties, writing a lot of books and learning to paint, sculp, compose music in my forties. However, when in my fifties, I began to devote my energies to becoming wise, the first bit of wisdom that came to me was that if I postponed my follies to my sixties I would probably be too old to enjoy them. So I switched and made my fifties my foolish years. I also came to realize that the key formula for being foolish was to say "Yes" and that for wisdom was to say "No."

So that is why, in my late fifties, when I got a phone call from Washington asking me if I would serve as this country's representative in speech pathology at the Pan-Pacific Conference on the Disabled to be held in Sydney, Australia, with all expenses paid, I said my automatic Yes. After hanging up the phone, I was appalled. I didn't want to go to Australia. Hell, I couldn't go. It was October; I was teaching four courses, doing research and therapy, and running my farm.

But I went, thanks to my wife who took over all my duties. She had been an instructor in speech pathology at the University of Minnesota before I married her.

Two weeks later, after a long trip by propeller plane via San Francisco, Hawaii, and the Fiji Islands, we soared in over Sydney harbor, a lovely sight.

Wearied to the bone, I went immediately to my hotel, a very ancient but luxurious one, took a bath in a tub so long I could lie down full length in it, then lay down on that great bed. The moment I got to sleep, however, the phone rang. It was Miss Grace Ellis, the queen of Australian speech therapy. She was to be my hostess, she said, and she would call for me at seven thirty to take me to the reception at the Governor's palace. It would be a black tie affair, she added. I told her I would come as I was, with a tie but not a black one and assured her I would also be wearing my coat and pants when I met her in the lobby. That produced a slight giggle.

A nice, very upper class and very British lady, we got along well throughout my stay but that reception for the delegates was tough on me. We milled around a big ballroom, holding champagne glasses, eating various delicacies including squid, making faces and small talk with strangers from many lands. By the end of an hour I felt as though I'd been inside a bass drum pounded by a hundred left handed drummers. It was no place for a man from Tioga and the forest. By the end of two hours I knew I'd have to get out of there or be a basket case so I told Miss Ellis I was leaving. "Oh, Dr. Van Riper," she said, "You can't possibly do that. We haven't even been through the reception line."

"The hell I can't," I replied, gave her my glass and bolted out of the front door of the palace into the night.

Fortunately there were some taxis there so I got into one and gave the driver a wad of Australian bills."Get me out of here fast and show me the town," I said.

"'You want girls, guv'nor?" he asked.

"Gad, no," I answered. "I just don't belong with those posh fancy pants. Take me to some of your pubs where I can see real people, real Australians, not British snobs. I'm an American and don't call me governor."

He laughed appreciatively. "Ok, matey,I'll show you the town and how the rest of us blokes have fun." After the first pub where we had some excellent ale and a waitress tried to sit on my lap, I was riding in the front seat with the cabbie, Joe, and we were boozum pals. Oh, what a fine night that was and I'm sorry I can't remember the details.

In one pub filled with sinister looking characters Joe told me how, during the war, he'd been with the Anzacs fighting the Germans all across Africa, and how, after they'd won, Winston Churchill came to review the troops as they marched past him still dirty and bloodied from the battle. And that,when old Winnie held up two fingers in the victory salute, all the Australian soldiers yelled, "Stick em up yer arse, Winnie; stick them up yer arse!"

Joe was a marvelous companion and I got a real education that night. He took me down to their long beaches where we waded, singing bawdy ballads. He liked my song about"Sammy Hall, Damn yer hide!"and joined me in the chorus. Once we got stopped by a policeman but Joe jollied him and invited him to join us as he showed this Yank the real Australia. I think the cop was tempted but he just grinned and waved us on.

I also vaguely recall Joe phoning the Minister of Fisheries at three in the morning asking him where I could catch a black marlin. Finally, he poured me back into my hotel and I slept until noon - or tried to.

I said tried to because every damned morning at precisely seven thirty a red haired maid, dressed in black with a white apron and a doily on her head, knocked on the door and opened it to bring me that awful coffee and cold toast and marmalade. Day after day I tried to dissuade her, once even getting on my knees to beg, but she said it was the custom of the house and that was that. I suspected that she might have had another occupation too because once, with a lewd wink, she told me I could have anything I wanted.

All I wanted was more sleep. Those Australians sure worked me hard the three weeks I was with them but I couldn't resent it because their therapists were so hungry to learn about our methods for treating all the speech disorders. After every talk I gave, and I gave many of them, they would bombard me for hours. They followed me back to the hotel, bought me drinks at the bar, and continued their probing. Lord, how they wanted to talk shop! But they were also very kind to me, drove me up into the gum forests of the Blue Mountains, and in Melbourne to a rain forest. They showed me cricket matches, jacaranda trees, kookaburra birds and kangaroos and in return I served as a consultant in their hospitals and clinics. They brought me their most difficult cases and asked for advice as to treatment. All in all, It was a fine experience but I was sure glad to get home.

When I went outside to feed the birds the contrast

between what I was seeing and the memory of sunny Australia was almost overwhelming. A blizzard was upon us and it looked as though it would be a bad one. In recent years we have had very mild winters compared to those we'd known in the past when great drifts of snow almost covered the farm bell. Driven by a very strong wind similar drifts were already forming. I thanked heaven for my snowblower and the plow on the John Deere and for John Eaton who would assuredly show up after work to open up the lane. Let it snow! I didn't have to go anywhere and the cupboards were full of food and whiskey. Time to play groundhog and hibernate. I spent the morning cooking and cleaning, even organizing my study which sure needed it, and as I did so I kept thinking of how we spent the winters in Tioga when I was a boy.

Although they were hard on my mother who hated our long winters with a passion and who, sometimes, would desperately scratch the windowpanes with her fingernails to remove the hoarfrost to see the pale sun, I always enjoyed that time of year. Just going to the barn to feed the horse and cow and to bring back an armload of wood was a challenge. I loved hearing the telephone lines singing in the wind, the squeak of my footsteps, the sparkling brilliant white that covered the land. Always carefully dressed for it with layers of woolen clothing, I do not recall ever being really cold though I suppose I was occasionally. When it got to thirty and forty below zero we rarely stayed outside long but I recall spitting through the mouth hole of my mask and seeing it explode in the icy air.

On milder days when the temperature remained at a minus ten or twenty for weeks at a time we had fun making caves and tunnels in the big drifts or even igloos when the snow was so packed you could cut blocks from it. Inside those caves it was always warm enough to have to shed a sweater or two. I recall once playing Eskimo and building a little fire in a can to roast my pretended whale blubber.

Of course we did a lot of skiing and sledding on our long steep hill street. When I was a small boy that street was never plowed. Instead, with two teams of horses, a huge log roller just packed down the snow. On the way down, one team with its driver would be behind the roller to keep it from running into the team ahead but returning up the hill both teams were in front. Because the roller was so large it made a hard surface where two vehicles could pass. No one shoveled the sidewalks except those to the houses and all of us walked in the roadway. I guess they still do.

But that fine hard surface was ideal for sledding. We kids could start at the crest of the hill near my father's hospital and whiz down to the railroad depot without ever having to push. Dragging the sled back up however was a chore unless we could hitch a ride on one of the big lumber sleighs. Someone in town had a long bobsled that would hold eight or ten kids and how we whooped all the way down.

We also did a lot of skiing, mainly cross country, though we always made a ski jump by Mt. Baldy or in the Company Field back of the grove. The latter also had one trail that went down through a large woods weaving through the trees and near its lower end to escape some big rocks you had to grab a certain sapling so you could make a right angled turn. I still carry in my groin a bit of dry fir branch that pierced it when I hung on a bit too long and straddled a dry spruce. It's a wonder any of us kids survived, the nutty things we did.

None of us ever learned to skate however, the snows were just too deep. One Christmas my grandparents sent me a pair of clip-on skates and I persuaded Fisheye and Mullu to help me clear a rink on Beaver Dam Pond. By the time we finished shoveling it was too dark to try and by the next morning it was covered by sixteen inches of new snow.

I remembered a lot of other things about my winters in the U.P. and only one of them was bad. It happened when I was perhaps seven years old. Surrounding our schoolyard was a fence built of iron pipes that had been discarded from the boilers up at the iron mine and one day an older kid persuaded me to lick one of those pipes. Of course my tongue froze to it instantly and I remained there stuck to it until a neighbor lady brought a kettle of hot water to release me. I still recall the pain of that skinned tongue and how I had only liquids for some days afterwards.

Yes, those winters were long but they were very happy ones and when spring came our joy was indescribable. "The crows are back! The crows are back! No, not ravens, crows I tell you!"

It sure had been a fine morning and a productive one. The house was clean, the potroast was bubbling in the crockpot, and I even did a washing. Four miles had been put on my exercycle and soon I would be in Mancelona en route to the U.P. If I could make it past this February I really would get there.

I slept well and after a quick lunch went after my mail plowing the drive with the John Deere as I did so. It was just too cold and blustery to walk though I felt guilty because I didn't. Two letters addressed to Cully Gage were in the box, one from a soldier in Saudi Arabia who was very homesick and said he'd brought along a copy of my Love Affair book to make his ordeal bearable. I wrote him a good long letter immediately telling him I was homesick too and that we'd both be back there eventually.

66

Then I opened the other letter. It was from a woman in Marquette who wanted some advice about how to write. "I can tell some good stories," she said, "but every time I try to put them down on paper I stall and they look terrible. How do you manage to write so easily and prolifically? What's the secret?"

I answered that letter right away too saying that being an author was never easy, that I labored hard in telling my tales, that I always had to revise and rewrite them before they satisfied me. My secret? I had no secret but over the years I had discovered a sort of procedure that helped me. It was this: First, I spent hours in mulling over the general features of the story while lying down. Oddly I've never been able to let my mind roam freely in any other position. Then, when I've got a vague outline of what I want to say and have some idea of how it would begin and end, I go to my typewriter and start pecking away, letting the tale just flow wherever it wants to go. I told her that I never looked at what I was writing or what I had written until it was, like peas porridge, nine days old. I've found that if I read it when writing it I become so critical Ican't continue. I told her I bet that might be part of her trouble, that she had to rid herself of her Censor. "You can always change the stuff you write later," I told her and said that she always should keep a certain person in mind as a prospective reader. I have several such people to whom I always tell my tales, one of them is young, the other an old gaffer like me but both are life long residents of the U.P.

Since she had said she never had enough free time without constantly being interrupted I told her I'd never had any either but I'd discovered how to solve that problem. I set myself a minimum quota of just one word a day. I could write many more of course and usually did but I demanded that one word to keep the writing going. Moreover, I never stopped my writing at a period but always left the sentence uncompleted. That way, the need for closure would enable me to return to the writing easily when I could get back to it again because I always knew what I had to say next. Well, that was the gist of what I wrote her before wishing her good luck and enclosing a little story that had taken me two days to write. Here's the tale:

Infidelity

In the tight little village of Tioga there was very little marital cheating mainly because everyone knew everything about everybody. There were no secrets in our town. Any hanky panky was certain to be discovered and spread all over town. For example, when old Mr. Belanger innocently had the gallantry to help Mrs. Deroche carry a heavy bag of groceries back to her house, the tongues wagged with speculation. Nevertheless, human frailty being pretty universal, some cheating must have occurred.

At the top of the long hill street in Tioga there's a gravel road that winds westward south of the old iron mine and when I was a boy we called that area Finntown. The last two houses on that road were owned by the Saari's and the Pikkunens. They were neat whitewashed log cabins and behind each of them was a cowbarn and a chicken coop. Between the barns sat a single log sauna which both families shared.

The couples were very good friends. In their late forties with their children long gone Down Below to make a living, they lived the good life of the U.P. Seppo Pikkonen worked on the railroad and Oscar Saari cut pulp for a living. With a cow and chickens, fish and venison, a big garden and enough biting money they never had any trouble making it through the winter. The two men hunted and fished together, helped each other make winter wood, and do other things while their wives sewed and canned and had coffee together every morning and afternoon. Yes, they were good friends, all four of them.

Curiously, the man and wife in each couple were unlike in personality, Oscar Saari being always happy and outgoing while his wife, Lempi, was more quiet and serious. The other man, Seppo Pikkonen, was very reserved but his wife certainly was not. A tall woman, still very attractive with long blonde hair and a merry eye, Thelma was always out for a good time, even occasionally being a bit flirtatious. Perhaps it was because opposites attract each other that the two couples enjoyed being together so much.

But things change. As many happily married men approach their fiftieth year a strange sexual restlessness comes over them and they start looking. Is it because they suddenly realize that they are getting old and want to recapture their fast fading youth? Now, such men start having affairs - or get divorced and marry some young girl in her twenties.

Not so in Tioga! Divorce was unthinkable and only the ugliest of young women would accept any wooing from an old geezer, then the word for any man over fifty.

When the folie de vieux, as our French Canadians called it, hit Oscar it hit him hard. No, he didn't look for a young girl; he knew better. Besides there was Thelma, right next door. Still possessing a fine figure and full of fun, he bet she'd be very lively in bed or haymow. Such thoughts made him feel very guilty and he tried to reject them but couldn't. Even when tamping down a tie on the railroad tracks the thought of her kept persisting. At night, with Lempi in his arms, he fantasized that she was Thelma and sex became exciting again. One evening the two couples attended one of the rare polka dances in the Town Hall and for weeks afterward Oscar kept feeling the thrust of Thelma's breasts against his chest. When she hung up the clothes on the line, he couldn't help ogling her. Yes, he had it bad. Then came a day when, as he went to fire up their joint sauna, he found Thelma inside scrubbing the benches. She teased him a little. "Oscar," she said,"You're supposed to hang up your clothes in the dressing room before coming in here." Unable to resist the impulse, he grabbed her and kissed her. Of course she slapped his face but not too hard and for a moment he thought she had kissed him back. Wahoo! Remembering the encounter, Oscar had hot pants for many days.

His ardor might not have been so strong had he known that over their morning coffee Thelma had told Lempi what had happened. Lempi was both shocked and furious. "Tonight I'll brain the old fool with a stick of stovewood!"

"No, no," replied Thelma. "You do that and he'd just beat you up. He'll come to his senses once he realizes he's not going to get anywhere with me. He's not my type, Lempi, and besides I love my quiet Seppo too much."

Having convinced himself that all he had to do was to proposition Thelma and make the necessary arrangements, Oscar did a lot of scheming in the days that followed. Somehow he'd have to get Seppo out of the way and Lempi too. Where would they go to bed and when? Sometimes his head ached from all the planning.

Finally he figured it out. It would have to be on Saturday night when both men usually went down to Higley's saloon for a few beers and to play cards with Laf Bodine and some of the other regulars. Pretending to get sick, he'd leave about eight o'clock and when he got home he'd tell Lempi he had the runs and would have to spend some time in the outhouse until they quit.Yah, that sounded reasonable.

He'd put some blankets on the loose hay and persuade Thelma to be there at exactly eight thirty. Yep, that should work. Half an hour would be long enough and no one would ever know.

To his delight, when he caught Thelma alone and outlined the scheme, she laughed and said sure, that she'd show him how to have some real fun in the haymow, that it was about time she had some variety.

And that next morning she told Lempi all about it!

Oscar found it hard to work the morning of the rendezvous

because he couldn't bend over without hurting himself. Even that afternoon when he took a hot sauna there wasn't any wilting.

After the hours finally passed the two men walked down the hill street to Higley's. Then, after a few beers, Oscar told Seppo he was feeling sick and thought he'd go home to bed. Seppo hardly noticed because he was winning big.

Looking at his watch when he got to his house, Oscar saw that it was exactly eight thirty so he went directly to the barn. He'd explain to Lempi later. Was she there? Yes, there was a big hump in the blankets. "You there?" he whispered hoarsely.

"Yah, I here," came the whispered reply. Tearing off his clothes, Oscar flung back the blankets. And there was his wife Lempi grinning at him.

At Happy Hour I read that tale to my deceased wife and she liked it. "It's a good yarn, Cully," she said. "I like that ending." So did I.

I didn't even go after the paper because it was still blowing and snowing so nastily. I was quite content just to sit by the fire. When it was time for supper I wished I had someone to share the potroast with because it was excellent. I had cooked it with Golden Mushroom soup, a tomato, an onion, and some carrots. Oh well, I could eat it another day or days and then make hash of it for the freezer. Perhaps John might come to help me get rid of it.

That evening I watched some nature programs on the TV and went to bed early. It had been another happy day. Poor Oscar!

DAY SIX

A lot of people have expressed surprise and shock when they find that I live alone at the age of 85. They ask, "What if something happens to you?" "What if you have burglars? Most frequently they ask me if I'm not terribly lonely. "Not at all," I tell them. "I have much company."

My first companion was my beloved Grampa Gage who joined me for breakfast even though he died seventy years ago. When he lived with us in Tioga I was only ten and he was my mentor and adult playmate. Every morning he would get me up early, shave himself and pretend to shave me, then make our breakfast before we set out on one of our crazy expeditions.

This morning I recalled one of those breakfasts. "Now, Mister O'Hare," Grampa said. (He always called me Boy or by some special name of the day.) "The common way to break an egg is to hit it with a knife or crack it against the edge of the frying pan like this." He demonstrated. "But life, Mister O'Hare, should be lived dangerously if it is to be at all interesting. Observe me carefully!" He picked up my egg, banged it hard against his long forehead, then emptied it into the pan. Not a trace of the egg was on his old noggin. "Well, Boy, that time I carried it off without getting a faceful and I'm proud I've begun the day this way. A bit of danger is the pepper in the stew of life. Not too much, just a little. Today you and I will explore the use of that condiment as we go about our business. Shall we play billy goat on Mount Baldy?"

Many years later, Grampa was with me again, this morning as I carved a thick slice of bacon. "Now cut it exactly a quarter of an inch thick, Boy, no less and no more. Them store bought bacon slices are always too skinny to cook right. Now sear both sides in high heat, then turn it down so it will cook slowly. Life and bacon are too precious to spoil them with hurry." Then when I was about to break this morning's egg, he spoke again. "Well, Boy, how about it?" I knew he was referring to living dangerously so I cracked the egg on my forehead after knicking it with my thumbnail as he had done so long ago. Eureka! There were only two little bits of egg shell in the pan and not a speck on my face. It would be a good day!

It was fun having Grampa with me as I fed the birds. I asked him how I could keep the varmints from eating all the sunflower seeds I'd put in the feeder. There was a big raccoon that had been swarming up the bird feeder pole every evening about dusk to tear off the top board of the bird feeder and gorge himself on the sunflower seeds. Night after night I'd watched him outwit all my efforts to thwart him. I'd greased the pole with vasoline; I'd put a latch on the cover which he soon learned how to unhook; I'd tied the cover on with rope which he immediately bit in two. In my desperation, I'd emptied the feeder and set a Havahart live trap baited with sunflower seeds and corn but the next morning, though the trap had been sprung there was no raccoon in it. Moreover it had been turned upside down and the seeds had fallen through the mesh and were all gone.

"Have you ever caught anything in that contraption? " Grampa asked skeptically. I told him I'd caught possums, skunks, woodchucks, birds, squirrels and rabbits galore, and even other raccoons but not this big one. I said I usually took them to the woods by the Boy Scout Camp down the road so the kids could hear things that went thump in the night.

"Ever get sprayed by a skunk?" Grampa asked.
"No, but John Eaton did and sure got polluted. He made the mistake of taking off the blanket covering the trap before opening the doors and the skunk came out with both cannons shooting. But Grampa, how come this coon springs the trap and gets away when the others don't?"

As always he gave the question some serious thought before replying. "I reckon he's such a big one the door falls on his rump and he just backs out." he said. "Coons are smart and you'll never get him to enter it again. Why don't you string a bit of the electric fence around the feeder pole, the fence you use around your garden to keep the varmints out?"

Of course," I exclaimed. For some years that fence had kept the woodchucks and coons and deer from eating my corn and melons. I hated to destroy it and the work might be hard. I'd have to dig up the posts, cut the wire netting, haul the battery and charger and use a heavy sledge to pound the rods into the frozen ground. That would be living dangerously indeed.

Nevertheless, with Grampa's help and counsel the project was completed. I found some extra rods, insulators, and wire in the horse stall and hauled the battery and charger in the cart behind the garden tractor. Lifting that battery was the hardest job and I had to sit down a spell but the ground wasn't frozen so deep I had to use the heavy sledge. Throughout all this activity Grampa was with me, advising, suggesting and offering bits of wisdom but all I can remember of the latter was "Slow and easy and never grunt!"

He also made the wise suggestion that I put a coil of wire right next to the feeder pole and laughed when I touched the completed contraption and yelped. I sure got a good jolt.

When the job was done I felt so tired and shaky I fell asleep on the davenport and when I awakened Grampa was gone. Still too tired, I decided to postpone my bicycle trip to the U.P. and to read while I had another "cup of jav" which is what we call coffee in the U.P. Selecting a book at random from the bookshelves in my study I came up with Sergeant's biography of Robert Frost which I hadn't read for years. Just inside the cover I found a message from Milove: "To Cul-ly a Merry Christmas for adding immeasurable poetry to my life for twenty six years .X X X K-Katy." I almost wept. She had spelled my name Cul-ly as my boyhood friends had pronounced it, not Cully, just as they always said win-ter instead of winter. She had also signed herself as K-Katy, a term I used when teasing her affectionately. Suddenly she seemed very near.

When I was a senior at the University of Michigan, Robert Frost was the "Poet in Residence", a position which gave him leisure to write. His only duties were to conduct one seminar in poetry each semester and I was one of the few students chosen to be in it. An unforgettable experience! Each student had to submit anonymously one poem a week and of them, Frost selected one or two he read aloud with his comments. Rarely did any of them get a favorable response and a few just made him mad. I recall how furious he became while reading the lines "The violin bow sucks music from the burnished wood." "Sucks, " he roared. "Sucks, Sucks, Sucks! "and then he went on to provide a wonderful account of the nature and appropriateness of words in poetic discourse, their sounds and rhythms. He told us of his own struggles to find the perfect word or phrase and how often he had chucked a morning's work into the wastebasket. Actually, Robert Frost used the seminar not for teaching nor for criticism but just to hear his own thoughts as he rambled on about anything that hit his momentary fancy. Privileged to watch and hear that wonderful mind at work, I often left the class dazed with exhilaration that lasted for hours.

About the middle of the semester a poetry contest was held with Robert Frost as the judge and after some self debate I entered it with this little poem:

Five of the Dryads were Foolish

(The aged Pan grew much weary of pipes and dancing and begged Zeus to grant him peace and quietness. Whereupon he was changed into a hidden pool in the forest. Aulus Gellius.)

Long years ago in lost Atlantis,

When Dryads danced in the woods,
A hidden pool in the orchard lay,
An ancient mulberry tree there stood
Gnarled and twisted, a grim old brute
Of the sylvan world, it shook its head
In grim defiance of all the dead
And every year dropped purple fruit
Into the pool that once was Pan.

Three great roots swam out and dived,
And in their bays great lilies grew.
White lilies, steeped in purple stain
Laughed in their cups and laughed again,
For once, long before, when the pool was new,
A band of dryads had stopped to drink
By the brink of the pool that once was Pan.
And the tree still grins a knotted old grin,
And laughs in the wind of evening skies,
For five of the dryads were foolish
But all of the lilies were wise.

Why Robert Frost picked that to win the poetry prize I don't know. I hadn't thought it was very good. Perhaps it was that the other entries were imitations of his work and mine was not. It did look better when it was printed in the Inlander, the University magazine, and brought me twenty five dollars and a roll of toilet paper inscribed "Poetic License" from my friend, John Voelker, who later became a Supreme Court Justice and the author of An Anatomy of a Murder. John and I drank the proceeds in bootleg whiskey and sang bawdy songs until dawn.

Anyway, Frost stopped me after class one day and asked to see other poems I'd written. Shy and overwhelmed by his interest I gave him only two, one of which "The Old Tailor" I later published in my book Tales of the Old U .P. He liked them too and said that if I could write enough others of the same quality he would help find a publisher. I had no other poems.

Moreover, several times that year Frost invited me to his home for a Sunday night supper of brown bread, beans and applesauce cooked by his wife Elinore, a lovely warm woman. The supper was always very good but the conversation was superb. Frost loved to talk and I don't think he ever said a dull word. He didn't like to be interrupted though, or to be asked questions. He preferred the monologue and, because of my stuttering, I was a very good and appreciative listener.

As I write this I'm tempted to insert the other poem of

mine that Frost liked and felt should be published. Oscar Wilde once said that the only way to get rid of a temptation was to yield to it so here it is:

Old Man Pone

Old Man Pon? That's me!
Pone's Dam" That's yonder.
Not a trickle snaking through.
Yeah, the sluice gate's been drawn up,
Just drawn her.
Dam full, say you?
That's my business too.
I don't squander
Water. Water don't come back.
When life and water leak away
They wander.

Looking sickly?
Ought to.
Not a bite inside my sack
For two days. Naw, got plenty food.
Belly's old and water logged.

See that crack?
Yeah, it's big but it's cemented good.
That's where my old pap, he stood
Keeping back
And sousing under dynamite
That farmers floated down on rafts
Things was black
That year - thirst and drought
Cattle died. They might
Have asked for water. Not them. No!
Bust your dam or we will!
Sure, a fight.

My pap, just a little slow...
Shocked him crazy. Shakes, you know.
Dirty sight!
Also made that crack you see
But Pone's Dam it held, you bet.
Been built right.

What's that tin case in the wall?
Case of fate, maybe.
You've good eyes to see that wire.

You get going, stranger. Quick!
You aint wanted. Git!

He'd better go. I'm no good liar.
Thirty feet of water creeping higher.
Soon I'll press upon this key
Before my own blood leaks away.
They'll get their water -valleys full.
Old God Pone. That's me!

I was so full of memories of the famous poet that he became my companion as I walked out to the back of my park. When I showed him the interior of the old barn he admired the great oak hand-hewed beams that supported the roof. He admired the adz marks. "The man who hewed those beams knew his craft," he said. "See how far apart those adz marks are. When I was a boy I made timbers too. Very satisfying, almost as good as creating a fine sentence."

Old Barn

Because I've painted it three times that old barn has held its color well on the front and sides but the back needs another coat because most of the paint is flaking off. I know I won't be able to paint it again. Frost looked at it a long time. "Reminds me of the face of an old apple farmer I knew in Vermont," he said." "Apple red spots of health on skin grey with age."

Frost talked continuously as we walked down the lane to

the pines and I wish I could remember all he said. Seeing tracks of rabbits and fox and raccoons in the new snow, he mentioned something about how all of us left tracks behind us and perhaps it was just as well that rain and snow would soon obliterate them. "Poems are tracks, too," he said, a bit sadly.

On our return I pretended to meet myself and said "Good morning, sir. It's a fine day." That made him chuckle. And when we came back to the house I was feeling so happy I just had to ring the old farm bell. When I did so, Frost said to me:

"Something there is in arms that wants to ring a bell,
To send a clang across the fields to hungry men
Or just to greet the stars or sun
Or just to say,' I am!'"

No one can be alone with Robert Frost as a companion.

It was almost noon when I entered the house and sat for a time in the big chair with the sun streaming through the big windows on my head. Old men should sit in the sun a lot. It warms the cockles of the soul. And the heart too. I'd worked too hard and was paying for it with some angina which went away after I took my little pill of dynamite, the nitroglycerin I always carry in my pocket. Soon the ache in my upper chest was gone so I took my nap. Usually when I do so I just rest but this day I slept deeply and felt refreshed when I awakened.

I ate my small lunch alone and enjoyed it. There are many times when I need no real or imaginary companions. Being alone means freedom, no demands upon you, no need to respond to the presence of others. It permits serenity.

Somehow I get the same feeling I knew as a boy in the forest. For some people solitude is unsettling. Once I brought a college friend up to the Old Cabin and when I left him there for a few hours he was almost frantic when I returned. "I can't bear the awful silence," he said. "I need people." Well, I like people too but I don't need them around me all the time.

Remembering the angina I rode down to the mailbox on the garden tractor, distributing some ears of corn for the pheasants whose tracks I'd seen there. Not much mail this time but at least there were two letters addressed to Cully Gage. I'd read them later.

That afternoon I had a series of imaginary companions, all of them from Tioga and my boyhood. The first one was Pete Half Shoes, the village's only pure blooded Chippewa Indian, who had meant so much to me at that time. He returned because I decided to make some rice pudding, being hungry for a sweet dessert that I hadn't had for weeks. Diabetics get these sudden hungers and the only way I've found to handle mine is by making applesauce or rice pudding heavily laced with some sugar substitute such as Sweet and Low. As I poured the rice out of the box I found myself wishing it were wild rice rather than the common variety. Long grained and much more tasty as well as more nutritious, it makes the best pudding but it's hard to find Down Below, at least in the stores John has searched. It was also hard to find in the U.P. but Pete Half Shoes knew of a little bay in Lake Tioga where it flourished. Once he let me go with him to get his winter's supply. After a long hike he found an old boat hidden in the brush and he laid an old blanket in its bottom. "Canoe better, "Pete said as he peeled two long sticks. "You pole and I show you."

As the boat plowed through the tall reeds and stalks it left a watery path behind us. With a stick in each hand, Pete, who was in the front of the boat, used one of them to bend the rice over its edge, then with the other stick tapped the stalks so the ripe grain fell onto the blanket.He sure was skillful as he alternately banged the grain first from one side of the boat, then from the other. There was a rhythm to it that when I tried I couldn't master. Pete didn't complain about my awkwardness, just patiently showed me again and again until I began to get the hang of it. Altogether we must have had about three quarts of rice in the blanket before we quit. That fine afternoon was seventy years ago but I recalled vividly the swish and flash of those shining sticks as we harvested that wild rice.

Another person with whom I spent some time that afternoon was Mr. Donegal, Old Blue Balls, the tough school superintendent who ruled us with an iron hand, ruler and strap. The memory of him had come with a fan letter from an old lady in the U.P. "I enjoy your stories very much," she said, "and especially those about Blueballs because we had a principal just like him who terrorized us. But you always describe him as being so hard and ferocious. Didn't he have a softer side? In your story about playing hooky, you told of how tenderly he cared for your friend that he rescued from drowning. He couldn't have been all bad."

Thinking to answer her, I had a hard time at first but then remembered the rainy afternoon when I was playing with his son, Halstead, in their attic. There were a lot of books up there and we had found one on the Vikings and their early settlements in America. It had some fine pictures of those Vikings and also of the Skelling, the Indians who eventually wiped out those who tried to live there.

Suddenly Halstead's father came up the stairs to join us and for almost an hour he told us tales of those early explorers, the runic stones that had been found as far west as Minnesota, the Viking artifacts that had been discovered in Massachusetts. And then he held us enthralled with an account of the glaciers that had shaped our land, lakes and streams long before the Indians arrived. Not once did he roar or seem formidable. He wasn't being a teacher; he was just having fun up there in the attic with us as the raindrops peppered the roof above. And when he left, he actually touseled our hair affectionately. Yes, I guess Old Blue Balls did have a soft side.

I made a cup of new coffee and wished I had some korpua to go with it but that was long gone. OK, I'd make some if I could recall how Rudi's mother, our common aiti, had done it years ago. She had cut thick slices of home made bread in half, lightly buttered both sides, sprinkled them with sugar and cinnamon, then baked them in the oven until they were very brown and dry. I didn't have any home made bread and had to use Sweet and Low but they turned out fine. I felt proud of myself but the best part was remembering that warm wonderful woman, my second mother, my aiti.

But my best companion of the day was of course Milove. Our Happy Hour lasted for two hours as we reminisced about the fine experiences we'd had together before the cancer hit her.

All in all it had been another almost perfect day even though I hadn't seen another person nor heard a human voice. No, I'm not a lonely old man. I'm a happy one.

DAY SEVEN

This day began with a phone call from Andy Amor, the husband of Elizabeth, my eldest granddaughter. "Sir," he said formally, "You are now a great grandfather." It didn't take long before he lost his cool as he excitedly told me that the baby's name was Peter and he weighed eight pounds and was beautiful and healthy and that Elizabeth was fine too and, and, and. "I'm a father" he exclaimed incredulously. "I can't believe it. What do I do now?"

I don't know what I told him but I went outside and shouted, "Hear ye! Hear ye! I hereby proclaim that this is Grandfather's Day, Great Grandfather's Day" and I rang the farm bell for five minutes before doing the Dance of the Wild Cucumber.

Of all the roles I've played in my long life, being a grandfather has been the most rewarding. Nine grandchildren have blessed that life, one after another, and in recent years after they grew into adults I've sorely missed the fine relationship I've always had with them. Oh, of course we're still close and I see them often but the best years of grandfatherhood are those when they're growing up. Now I could be a grampa again.

After that first fine exhilaration ebbed, I had the sobering thought that I probably wouldn't live long enough to be that Grampa to Peter, Peter the Great. The hell I wouldn't! Now I had another reason to survive despite the odds. I'd not only get back to the U.P. but I'd also play with a great grandson, no matter what!

So many memories flooded me that I found no interest in doing anything else. Nuts with doing the washing I'd planned! No, I wouldn't get a much needed haircut or my beard trimmed. The letters I'd planned to write could wait. For once I regretted living alone and not being able to share the good news. It would be silly to phone a friend and announce that I had become a great grandfather. They wouldn't understand what it meant to me. Ah, finally I found a solution to my dilemma. I'd write my son-in-law, Ben Krill, Elizabeth's father, and tell him about the joys of being a Grampa. I spent the whole day writing it and here it is:

To A New Grandfather

So you've just become a new grandfather. Welcome to the

clan! Being a father was fun but being a grandfather is even better mainly because you and your grandchild share a common enemy, the generation in between. Now you can have all the pleasures without any responsibility, Now you can be a child again.

Some say that all newly born infants are just blobs or that they all look like Winston Churchill, that until they learn to bang a cup or walk or talk they just aren't very interesting. I have not found it so. Each of the nine grandchildren with whom I've been blessed has fascinated me even in that first year more than my own children ever did. No two of them were alike. One would gurgle in contentment when I held it in my arms; another would burp or yawn; still another would wail or wet his pants. All of them would curl their tiny fingers around my thumb and not let go. You'll like that.

Many new grandchildren stare at you and their confusing world with a rather dazed expression as if to say, "What the hell is all this, Grampa?" When they do, you must say, "Child, what you're seeing doesn't make much sense, does it? It never will, but that beautiful woman over there is your mother; that man making silly faces is your father, and I, with the white whiskers, am your loving Grampa. Now that the formal introductions are over, you may go to sleep." The baby never does. It just lets out a wail and its mother hurriedly grabs it away from you. That's all right too.

As a grandfather you may occasionally be privileged to feed the baby - from the bottle, not the breast. You won't be as awkward as you were when your own children were little and if your arthritic elbow makes you call for Grandma after ten minutes, so be it. Fortunately you won't be able to see the fatuous expression on your face. Grandfathers always look a bit silly when feeding babies their bottles. Grandmothers don't. Remembering, they look beautiful.

When I was a boy in Tioga, I often visited the home of one of my Finn friends, Ted Koski. His ancient grandmother, a tiny and very ugly old woman was always rocking herself in a chair next to their kitchen range as she smoked a blackened corncob pipe or sipped coffee through a sugarlump held between her toothless gums. Her face had wrinkles on its wrinkles and resembled a withered dry apple. Yet once I saw the old lady holding her eleventh grandchild against the nipple of a bottle and her face held a beautiful, most ethereal expression. I've never forgotten it. We men can never look like that.

I hope you'll be better at burping babies than I have been. Oh, I could sling them over my shoulder correctly but I couldn't bear to thump the bonnie little bugger hard enough to evoke the belch that was needed. I've read that in Arabia the dinner guests must express their appreciation of the meal by loud and frequent belchings and burpings. When they were six months old, all my grandchildren were Arabs. I hope you'll be a better baby burper than I was.

Once your grandchild begins to explore the delights of solid food, including its use as a shampoo, you can witness again the wonderful achievements of learning to talk and walk. One of my nine crawled backwards; another crawled only in circles; another didn't crawl at all - just stood up one day and walked. Now you can witness again what our prehistoric ancestors discovered when they realized they didn't have to go on all fours. Homo erectus! No wonder the baby squeals triumphantly when he pulls himself up vertically, sidles along the davenport, and toddles into your waiting knees. Wahoo! I hope you'll yell in triumph too. I did - nine times!

Similarly you can again watch homo erectus become homo sapiens as your grandchild learns to talk, the greatest achievement of mankind. When your own children were babies you probably missed that miracle. Now you can witness each phase of the learning.

Most mothers insist that their children learned to talk about the time of their first birthdays or shortly thereafter, but that's not true. Throughout all that first year they are mastering the basic skills necessary for speech, yes, even when crying. As a father you probably disliked, perhaps even resented, that squalling especially in the wee hours of the night but to have speech you have to learn how to make sounds. As a grandfather, you'll find it interesting rather than unbearable. You'll observe him crying both on inhalation and exhalation, then settling on the latter. You'll watch him crying with his legs keeping time to his wails, and that most of the latter are nasalized vowels. Kipling claimed that he could distinguish an Oriental from an Occidental cry of pain, that we of the western world cry "Ow!" whereas the Oriental wails "Ai, ai, ai." Listening, the thought may come to you that your grandchild must have a Chinese ancestor on his mother ' s family tree. But don't try to figure out why he's crying. That's for mothers or grandmothers. Buhler, a famous researcher in child development, once listed ten different conditions that made a baby cry, among them hunger, wetness and uncomfortable postures, but there's an eleventh cause too. Sometimes a baby just cries for the hell of it. So enjoy and call Grandma.

Watch for the comfort sounds, Grampa, because they are

the real beginnings of speech. Out of them will come the repeated syllables of babbling when he plays with his mouth much as he does with his toes . He's practicing so don't interrupt or he'll quit. Just enjoy that fairy music while it lasts for soon he will be stringing syllables that almost seem as though he's trying to tell you something . "Gobba me ma ma?" he may seem to be asking as he experiments with the inflections of questioning or of command. One of my grandchildren demanded "Bahba bahba bahba " when she didn't have enough hair to ruffle a brush. It's fun watching your grandchild learning how to speak.

And it's even better when do they start using meaningful words. Alas, I'm afraid they won't be saying "Grampa" for some time, That "Gr" blend involves too many tough coordinations, They'll use the easy sounds like those made with the lips or tongue tip, the m,p,b,w, and t and d sounds, along with various vowels to say such early words as "Mama","Dada," or "wa-wa" for water. Yet, one of my granddaughters first words was "pitty" (pretty) a comment on a flower I'd given her. Don't insist that they imitate you. Just provide the word as a model when it is needed. And make it easy for them by speaking simply and in short phrases or sentences.

The best years of grandparenthood start when they are half past three or four years of age, when you can assume the role of an adult playmate. These are the lap years, the hugging years, the years of unconditional love. You may have forgotten how good it is to have a child squeal with delight when you come through the door, to have him grab your legs and beg to be held instantly. "Gampa, Gampa, " he'll whisper in your ear . "I lub you. "

Soon will come the years when the child will want to walk hand in hand with you in exploring the wonders of the outside world, so take little steps. Holes in the ground, bugs, big and small, the feel of tree bark, the sound of birds, all these are new experiences to be shared by both of you. To see these things is to be reborn, to be a child again. I hope both of you can find a Secret Place to have as your very own - even if it's only a spot behind a special tree. There you can answer his questions: "Gampa, why do I have only two fumhs?" "Gampa, will I be as big as you someday? " "Kin I see in your gwasses? "

There in your Secret Place you can invite him to find the Secret Pleasure of the day, the two mints you've hidden in your pocket . As he swarms over you, you'll hear that wonderful giggle of discovery and you may find yourself giggling too. And, as you eat your mints, you can sing, "Oh a little bit of candy makes the medicine go down/ the medicine go down/ the medicine go down/ Oh, a little bit of candy makes the medicine go down/ in a most delightful way. " Children love to have you sing to them and don't mind a bit if your old voice crackles . He'll also squeal with delight if you do some rhyming. When his shoe falls off, as boy's shoes always do, you can chant, "Johnny lost his shoe/Boo hoo hoo." Then, of course, you must take off your own shoe and throw it for him to retrieve as you both chant, "Gampa lost his shoe/Boo hoo. ."

Feel Grampa's Beard

Beneath your dignity? Oh, come on! It's about time you lost the barnacles of inhibition that have covered your keel. It's time you learned how to play again. Let that grandchild of yours teach you how to enjoy the present moment to the hilt and nuts to the past or future. You're a grampa now, with a licence to be foolish.

How many fine memories I have of those days with my own grandchildren! Even the furniture of this old house reminds me of them. This big recliner chair with the wooden arms was the focus of many good moments. It was my chair, Grampa's chair, and woe to any little kid who tried to preempt it, as they well knew. So, of course, whenever I entered the room there was sure to be a giggling little scamp sitting in it, eyes sparkling with anticipation. "Who's in my chair?" I'd roar and then, snorting ferociously, chase the kid around the davenport. Or I'd pretend I hadn't seen him and sit down carefully, jump up startled and chase him around again. Because I couldn't bear to throw it away, I still have a wide rubber band on the arm of that chair which we used to play "Snap Grampa." The grandchild would lift up the band while I inserted my forefinger under it, then the kid would chant "M.B.G. One, two, three" and let the rubber band snap down on my finger as I tried to pull it out of danger. Often I didn't and then I'd howl in mock anguish and chase the merry little devil around the dining room table. That M.B.G. means Monkey Business Grampa and even now when they are thoroughly mature their letters always begin with the salutation: "Dear M.B.G." Another honorary degree!

Grandchildren love magic in any form. I have a few tricks such as being able to make a coin disappear up my sleeve but the one they loved best was when I'd say the magic word, then pull out my upper denture and pretend to bite them with it when they fled..Then I'd tell them that if they could say that magic word, they could pull out their teeth and bite me too. Oddly enough. though they tried hard, they were never able to say it correctly, perhaps because it's just a jumble of connected sounds like "eeligochamasikaveronaput."

When the holidays come and all of your grandchildren are assembled I suggest that you get them all worked up and rowdy by playing "Follow Grampa." Line them up in a row and lead them all over the house doing nutty things like crawling on all fours, waving your arms, hopping on one foot, putting your head between your legs, or doing my Dance of the Wild Cucumber. When they're really war-whooping and climbing the walls, you discreetly get the hell out and let their parents calm them down.

They will want to sit beside you at the dining room table , of course, and if they happen to drop a spoon you must also drop yours, and perhaps your knife and fork as well. Great hilarity! Once when my grand daughter Julie spilled her whole mug of milk on the floor, I spilled mine too much to the irritation of her grandmother who had to clean up the mess. "You've gone too far, Cully," she said disapprovingly but Grampas can never go too far.

But there are also the quiet times when your grandson will crawl up into your lap and say, "Grampa, read me a book or tell me a story." I suggest that you do the latter because most children's books are pretty terrible. What I usually did was to pretend to read from The Upside Down Book, making up a wild tale in which the child plays an important role. Using their own names seems to intrigue them as they hear about what they did to the crocodile on the River Nile or something such. Even as adults they still recall some of their adventures that came from the Upside Down Book. Never shush them when they interrupt or ask questions but answer them very seriously after due thought. About the only problem you may encounter comes when they demand you tell the same story again because they want it told in exactly the same way. "No, Grampa. That's not right. My froggy jumped on the table first and then he jumped up into the tree." You won't find it hard to make up these tales if you're still a child at heart. Grampas are! Alas, this wonderful period does not last forever. Like you, your grandchildren will be growing older. They find other interests, other playmates. Then what they want is not a playmate but a companion or a teacher though not like those they have in school. They hunger to learn the things big people do, especially those that their own parents can't or don't teach them.

At the crucial ages of from nine to eleven I was very fortunate to have my Grampa Gage living with us and in my Northwoods Readers I've written much about our companionship. After we'd had our early breakfast and were sitting on the back steps in the sun he'd say, "Mister McGillicuddy, what, sir, do you suggest we do this fine morning?" Grampa never talked down to me; he always listened gravely to what I said; he never preached. Often he'd ask me to help him on some little job such as hoeing the beets or picking strawberries and always thanked me for my valuable assistance. He made me feel grown up, an equal, a cherished companion. My own father had neither the time nor the inclination to play such a role but Grampa seemed to know what I needed - the opportunity to identify with a real man.

I cannot number the things he taught me. Indeed, he never seemed to he teaching but rather just watching me learn. For example when I was learning how to fly fish and my line kept falling in coils at my feet to my utter frustration, he put an apple on a stick and bade me fling it off. That was all. No instruction, no demonstrating, but I got the idea and soon was casting my trout fly with ease. A good woodsman, he taught me much about nature without ever seeming to teach. He sought my aid in making his collections of rocks, tree bark, flowers, animal tracks, and even smells. We roamed the forest and streams exploring their delights together and almost incidently I learned that we Gages didn't lie or cheat and that we coped with adversity or disappointment with grace. And, most of all, to have the gay spirit, and enjoy every moment. I have an unbounded imagination and Grampa had one too. "Sir," he'd say to me on Mount Baldy, "We're badly outnumbered. We've got to retreat before those Philistines kill us. Get on your horse and we'll escape them." Then both of us would mount our sticks and gallop down the hill to fight another day. At various times we'd be chickens laying eggs, Bushmen hunting lions in Africa or a bird flying over our town and lakes. Last summer I visited Our Elephant, a huge granite boulder that we tamed and rode more than seventy years ago. Grampa knew my need for fantasy and encouraged it. I have done so too with my grandchildren as I hope you will with yours.

During this preadolescent period your grandson will also need you as a confidant. I told my Grampa Gage things I'd never tell my parents. As a grandfather, I've been honored to share the private thoughts and feelings of all nine grandchildren. Sometimes I've almost felt like a priest hearing confession though the sins are small, small sins. Always I gave immediate and absolute absolution - but no penances. And I never told!

The situation with your granddaughters will be different. Unlike the boys, they cannot and do not want to identify with you. They need grandmothers to be their companions and confidants, grandmothers who need their help in baking cookies and going shopping. There's no need to feel jealous. That's just the way things are.

Having found that granddaughters love to get mail, I've maintained a close relationship with them by correspondence (with each letter of course addressed to Miss). The crazier the letter, the more they like it! Often all I sent them was a bit of mildly bawdy doggerel: "Dear Miss Jennifer Ann Squires: I have a poem for you today. 'Jennifer Ann/Jennifer Ann/Did a big dirty in the frying pan/Did it twice That wasn't nice/ Jennifer Ann, Jennifer Ann, Your loving Grampa."

A few years later, when they've discovered that boys have legs, I write them wild love letters from imaginary admirers. Occasionally they may answer: "Dear MBG: My dog has fleas and bites herself. School is OK, I love you."

It's always a bit hard when in their adolescence they leave you for a time. You'll go to their high school programs and plays and watch them parade in the band or compete in sports and feel good if they wink or wave at you but the old intimate relationship will be gone. They won't need you but you can enjoy watching them grow. And if you're as lucky as I am, there will come a time when their husbands or wives will phone you and say "Hello, Great Grandfather."

Well, that's what I wrote to Elizabeth's father - and perhaps for all grandfathers. With breaks for lunch, my nap, the mail and some walks it took me all day. I was very tired by Happy Hour until a good fire on the hearth restored me. Yet I couldn't get my own grandfather out of my head and thought of my disappointment when the Averys, my publishers, rejected a tale I wrote for the most recent Northwoods Reader,"And Still Another." The story was called "Grampa Tells Me About Sex". I thought I had handled the touchy subject with some delicacy but they sure didn't. They said it would offend too many readers.

After some search I found a copy of the tale and read it again. Yes, they were right and Milove would have agreed with them. Yet it was a good tale and a true one. Perhaps I could delete the objectionable material. After a lousy frozen fish dinner I tried revising it and here it is:

Grampa Tells Me About Sex

For some reason I had overslept that morning and as I went down the back stairs to the kitchen I heard Mother talking about me to Grampa so I listened. "Cully's almost eleven, Father," she said, "and soon he'll be adolescing. He needs to have some good information about his sexual urges but when I asked his father to do so, he refused. I don't know why. You and Cully have such a close relationship I know he'd listen to you. Please!"

"Aw, Edith," Grampa replied. "That's a crazy idea. Why don't you tell him yourself?"

"Please, Father! Please!" She knew he'd do anything for her.

"Well, I'll think about it," he replied. I could tell he wasn't enthusiastic. Behind the door I was grinning, thinking it should be an interesting morning.

After I'd had my belated breakfast, Grampa and I sat on the back steps for a spell making our plans for the day. "Mr. McGinty," he said. "I would appreciate your reaction to my proposal that we go up to make a cave on Mount Baldy. You know those two big slabs of rock on top of the east slope. By putting a roof of branches across them we can have our cave. We need one up there. Those sabre toothed tigers are always prowling around and a little coffee fire at the entrance will keep us safe. What do you say to that, Mr. McGinty?" I joyfully agreed.

As we passed Sliding Rock Grampa began telling me about Pre-his-toric Man. (He always sounded out the big words for me.) From what he told me those early ancestors of ours must have had a rough time surviving. They didn't even have bows and arrows, Grampa said, just spears and stone axes. They were always hungry and ate grubs and worms when they couldn't kill any game. They had no real clothing, just animal skins. Dangers lurked everywhere. "No point to trying to climb a tree when a sabre toothed tiger comes after you," Grampa said. "Hell, them varmints can climb a tree quicker than you can spit. Hey! What's this?" He pointed to an indentation in the path. "Danged if that aint a tiger track, Boy! We'd better be making our cave in a hurry so we can make a fire in the opening and be safe. The one thing those sabre toothed tigers is scared of is fire."

We climbed the bluff and frantically began covering the

space between the two big rocks with branches. They looked a bit flimsy. I was beginning to believe some tiger would soon be getting our scent and so I was relieved when the job was done and we had a little fire at its entrance. Grampa pulled out his pipe and we sat there safe but listening intently. Then he broke the silence. "Boy," he said, "before we go outside to make ourselves some spears and stone axes I want to ask you some questions. First, let me say to you a little poem. 'The flea is wee and mercy me/ You cannot tell the he from she/ But she knows well/ And so does he.' Now my question is this: What's the difference between a male and a female, between a boy and a girl?"

I wanted to say that boys had peckers and girls did not but, hating to use that term, I used my mother's word. "Boys have wee wees and girl's don't," I replied.

Grampa was both shocked and outraged. "Don't you ever say that baby word again!" he roared. "A male has a penis, a dong. A ding dang dong is what makes a man a man. It's his proudest possession, Boy!"

Grampa lit his pipe again. "I presume, Boy, that you know why you have a penis?"

"Yes sir," I answered, "to pee with."

"That's true, Grampa said gravely," but it's also used for fornication. Do you know what that means?"

"Yes," I replied. "You taught me that word last year when Puuko, our cat, was going out screwing every night. I began to recite his poem that had the word in it: "Cats on the housetops/ Cats on the tiles/ Cats with syphilis...."

Grampa hurriedly interrupted me. "Oh dear me," he said. "I'm a dirty old man corrupting the youth of the land." He puffed on his pipe a long time before he continued. "I presume also that you have occasionally witnessed the act?"

"Yes, sir," I said. "Roosters do it; dogs do it; so do chipmunks. I've even seen squirrels do it upside down on trees. And last year Dad asked me to lead Rosie, our cow, over to the Salos so their big bull could service her. Wow! Was that something! She bellered all the way home. "Grampa, how do birds do it?"

"Damned if I know," he replied. "I suppose they do it with their feet on the ground or on a branch. Seems like it might be difficult to do on the wing." "But dragon flies do it when flying," I protested. "I've seen them, one on top of each other in the air."

"Mebbe so, mebbe so. Seems like you know more about fornication than I do. How the hell did I get into this anyway?" Grampa lit his pipe again.

I told him how Fisheye and I had once seen Mr. Hummel's stallion on top of a mare in their barnyard. "It was scary, Grampa," I said. "He was snorting like crazy and when he mounted the mare he bit her on the neck too."

"How about fish?" Grampa asked.

"Oh, I know all about that," I replied. "Mullu and I spent a whole Saturday afternoon watching a gravel bed in Beaver Dam creek where a big female trout scooped out a hole in the sand with its tail and laid some yellow eggs in it. And then a smaller trout came by and squirted some white stuff over the nest. Then she chased him away and started fanning the eggs with her tail. Interesting!"

"So you know all about sperm and eggs." Grampa seemed impressed.

"Oh yeah,"I answered. "All females have eggs in them just like hens do but the eggs don't have any shells on them while they're still inside. I cleaned a chicken once and the eggs were soft and yellow. Boys don't have eggs in them, do we?" Grampa shook his head.

"Grampa, why do some of the eggs turn out to be boys and other eggs girls? I tried to find out by looking in Dad's medical books when he was out on a house call but it was too full of big words. They had some interesting pictures, though."

"Lord, I don't know why some eggs become male and others don't,'" he replied. "What kind of pictures have you seen?"

"Oh, there's one book that shows how babies grow from the very first when they're inside the mother.There's a picture of something looking like a tiny tadpole entering the egg. Then the egg splits in two, then it becomes an embyro."

"No, not embyro. It's embryo, em-bree-o. " Grampa seemed happy to contribute to my fund of knowledge.

"OK, embryo. Anyway, they're sure ugly at first, all big head and belly and with tiny arms and legs all curled up. I think it said that at eight weeks it was only about an inch long. Is that true?"

Grampa didn't answer.

"I saw a baby being born once," I continued. "Right on our front porch. Surprised everybody, I guess. No one noticed I was watching as Dad pulled it out until after he had cut the cord.Then he saw me and asked me to go fetch a pail from the shed so he could put the afterbirth in it. And then he told me to bury it in the rhubarb patch. Some kids think that babies are brought by the stork or come in the doctor's satchel. They're nuts!"

"That rhubarb pie we had yesterday was the best one I

ever ate," mused Grampa. "Let's go home, Boy. Let's go home."

As we again passed Sliding Rock I thought of something else. "What's the missionary position, Grampa?"

Again he just shook his head and didn't answer.

****

Well, with that expurgated version of a better tale I called it quits. It had been a great grandfather's day indeed.

DAY EIGHT

It was another nasty day when I stuck my head outside the back door. Sleet and a very hard wind would keep me confined to the house. Where was the spring that the calendar said should be here? Refusing to yield to negative or depressive thoughts, I vowed that I would make the day a good one. "Enjoy! Enjoy!" Grampa had commanded. So I enjoyed my grapefruit-mit-bananas, the cinnamon toast and coffee and the smoke rings circling upward from my pipe. What should I tackle on this, another fine day in the life of Cully Gage?

Well, I could start by mending Mullu whose stem I had broken yesterday. All of my pipes are named after friends and Mullu is a long time favorite. Somewhere in my study is a box containing bowls and stems of broken pipes that I've gathered over the years because I've always found it difficult to discard an old friend. Perhaps in the box I could find a stem that would fit Mullu.

I never did find that particular box but I found another that had once held typing paper. It was labeled "The Impossible Dream." I laughed aloud when I saw it because I knew it contained the last remains of my crazy attempt to become a composer of Flame Symphonies. I was still grinning at the memory of my wife's reaction when, at a Happy Hour fire, I told her what I was intending to do.

"Madam, Milove," I said. "Your loving husband is about to embark on a new project. I am..."

She interrupted. "Oh no" she wailed in alarm. "No more mynah birds. No more pigs to eat my flowers."

"No, nothing like those," I answered. "I've had this idea for years and it first came to me when I was sitting by a campfire up at the Hayshed Dam. I'm going to try to become a composer, the first composer of symphonies using flames rather than musical notes."

She giggled a little. "Cully, you're having your midlife crisis a bit early but it sounds harmless enough. At least you aren't planning to chase some younger woman."

"Lord, no," I replied. "One woman like you is enough for any man but listen to me. I know it sounds crazy but think of the possibilities.There hasn't been a new art form in ten thousand years. It will be the poor man's art form. With some wood, a match and my directions he could build a fire that would have a prelude, a theme with variations and a grand finale."

Watching our own fire burning on the hearth she tried to

keep a straight face. "Cully, the Mozart of the Flame. You promised me that I might have a rough time after I married you but that I would never be bored. You were correct, Milord."

"Oh, but there's much more to it," I said. "This new art form will not only have the sounds of the fire but also the colors and shapes and movements of the flames. It will combine music and painting and sculpture and even the dance because flames are never still."

Not trying to suppress her mirth any longer she said, "Excuse me but I'd better start supper. Picasso, Rodin, John Sebastian Bach and Fred Astaire will be eating my meatloaf tonight." As she left for the kitchen there was a strange smile on her face. Even now, forty years later, I can still see that smile.

In the box that contained the notes of this project I found some of the cards on which I had identified the colors of the flames. I remembered thinking that to go about the project systematically I should begin with something easy like identifying the colors and finding words or symbols to represent them but this proved very difficult. There were blue flames, yellow flames, grey flames, orange flames, even green ones but most flames were none of these. They were flame colored and no other term could describe them any better than that. OK, I'd use the letter F as their symbol and perhaps find a better one later.

Composing Flame Symphony

As I sat there on the stool by the fireplace recording the flame colors I asked my wife to help me. "What would you say is the color of that flame on the extreme right?" I'd ask and she'd answer "oriental poppy" or "custard pie." Not much help, terms like that. And one time when I was in the bathroom I heard her calling me, "Cully, come quick. There's a black flame." A black flame? I'd never seen one, nor ever a pink or purple flame either. Tugging up my pants I tore into the living room.

"Sorry, it's gone," she said. "Do you know what the date is today?" It was the first of April. Somehow I began to have the impression that she wasn't taking my project very seriously.

Another unexpected problem was that the color of the flame often depended on the kind of wood that was burning and varied with the position of the wood and the duration of the fire. For example, wild cherry yielded more blue flames than any other wood; horizontal logs had more blue flames than slanting ones; more blue appeared as the logs were just beginning to burn, then turned to yellow or flame color later. Grey flames were ghost flames, disembodied from their source and floating unattached. Green ones were rare and tended to occur in the transition between the blue and yellow. Things were getting complicated but the more I watched my fires the more intrigued I became. I had watched a thousand hearth and campfires in my time but now I was seeing things I'd never seen before.

Finally I felt I had pretty well mastered the problem of color and to test that belief I got up early one morning and laid a fire on the hearth consisting of a lot of different kinds of wood: pine, cedar, pale oak, hickory and even sassafras, arranging them carefully and writing down in my notes a prediction of the colors that would ensue when I lit it that evening.

When I did so I was met with the damndest display I'd ever seen. All the colors of the rainbow flared. I looked accusingly at my wife. "You've sprinkled some of those powders," I said angrily.

"Yes, " she said."Since you're more interested in those flame colors than you are in me I thought I'd give you a real dose of them. Cully, you worry me. You're becoming obsessed. I'm getting so I dread Happy Hour. You never talk to me but just sit on that stool watching the fire and taking notes." Of course she was right so I took a few weeks off and gave her a lot of loving attention.

Later that month, however, I was at it again, this time listening and analyzing the music of the flames.The variety of sounds I began to hear almost overwhelmed me. There were crackles, pops, ticks and tocks. There were spluts from a flatulent fire. Occasionally I heard a loud report similar to that produced by a rifle shot so loud it almost jumped me off my stool.

If I had a piece of wood that wasn't thoroughly dried it would whistle or hiss, sometimes so high in pitch it was barely discernible. The best of this fire music tended to occur early as the kindling and small wood caught fire. When the fire died down there were rustles and sizzles and periods of complete silence.

Some woods produced more sounds than others, especially dried spruce and cedar. Again I had great difficulty finding symbols for these sounds and finally just used descriptive words. Once, when I was trying to imitate some of these sounds, Milove said to me "Pop pop, tick, crackle, ssss, and splut, splut, splut," so I quit building fires for three months in the interest of my domestic tranquility.

When I began again it was with sparks and they almost made me despair. There were single sparks, usually following a loud pop, that zigzagged their way up the flue. There were doubles and twins and when a log shifted a shower of them would always appear. Some sparks died almost instantly; others found a short resting place on the back wall of the hearth, often creating patterns. Once, when a shower created a pattern that resembled the profile of a human head, I asked my wife if she saw it too.

"No," she replied. "All I see is the profile of a man I used to know - my husband."

I realized that a composer of flame symphonies must not only be a painter and use colors, or a musician and compose with tones. He also had to be a sculptor because he had to deal with the varying shapes and contours of the flames. Could it be done? Calder's mobiles came to mind. They too constantly changed. Were there any words to describe these shapes and contours? Yes, there were sheets of flame, flames that curled, single flames that bounced. Often at the base of a log a long series of short flames lined the lower surface looking like yellow teeth. OK, I'll call them teeth. Some flames merely flickered; others flowed continuously. There were flares and bursts of flame. Some flames were forked; some had a single apex. We kept horses back then and often to relieve my frustration I'd go out to clean their stalls.

When I started on the final phase of my project, the recording of the movements of flames, I was beginning to get a bit tired of the whole damned thing. It meant that I would have to learn the choreography of the dance, something I knew absolutely nothing about. Flames did dance; they were rarely still. How could I possibly record them? When I asked my wife to find a book on choreography at the library she flatly refused.

"But won't you be glad to be able to say that you're the

wife of the inventor of flame symphonies?" I asked teasingly.

"Perhaps," she answered. "but then the attendant at the State Hospital will say that you are in the third cell on the left, the one with the barred windows. And that when he gets the keys he'll let me see you for a few minutes."

So I never did manage to orchestrate my flames. Instead I decided to try to put together all that I'd learned and seek to create my first flame symphony. With great care I prepared the series of sheets on which I recorded the colors and sounds and shapes of what I would find once I set fire to the carefully placed kindling and logs. There was a sheet for each ten minutes and it was covered with symbols and words that would make no sense to anyone else but me.

Before I lit my masterpiece, and following the scores frame by frame, I told my wife exactly what would happen, how the prelude produced by my kindling would look and sound. I described the shapes and contours she should look for in the major theme and its variations. I presented a word picture of my grand finale. Then with a flourish I lit the match.

Ach du lieber Augustine! Gage Flame Symphony Number One was an utter flop, a disaster. Nothing I'd predicted came true. Indeed only half of my kindling caught fire at all, No blue flames appeared on the lower surface of my cherrywood triangle. The forked flames did not lick upward along the short upright chunk of oak but spread sideways instead. The osage orange slab that was supposed to create a great shower of sparks for the finale caught fire instantly and fell off to one side. My back log of maple never did flame, not even when I dumped all the sheets of my symphony on top of it. There were few embers.

And Milove laughed and laughed. So did I.

Back to the drawing board? No! I'd done my damndest; angels could do no more. I packed up my notes and hid them in the study. I've built a thousand fires since but never attempted another flame symphony. Was it worth it? Of course. It's the seeking, not the attaining of an impossible goal that counts. I now know how to watch a fire and my pleasure in doing so is much greater than it ever was before.

Like old buggers from the U.P., impossible dreams are hard to kill and when at last they do die, new dreams arise from their humus. That happened this afternoon.

No, I'd never try to compose another flame symphony but why not try to make a videotape of a fire from start to finish. Now we had color photography. Now we had a way to preserve a fire and enjoy it time and time again. I have two cherished video cassettes, one of wolf music and the other of ocean waves that I treasure and replay often. Each has some commentary which interprets what I am seeing and hearing. Why not try to do the same for a hearth fire?

I borrowed a Camcorder from a friend, built a good fire, photographed part of it, then played it back on my TV while adding my commentary. I felt the old excitement welling up inside me. Yes, it could be done and I could do it. Now all those poor souls who had no fireplace in their homes or apartments could have the joys of fire watching. What a market! If the first video cassette sold well, I could follow it with another and even better one. Oh, I'd have to learn how to edit my shots and commentary to keep them within the necessary time limits but that could be done. Now I'd have a new project for my old age and have some further impact on others I would never know in person.

When I told Milove about it at Happy Hour she laughed outrageously and told me to look up the story "Flame Symphonies" in my first Northwoods Reader to see how my father had reacted.

I'd forgotten all about that tale in which I told about Carl Anters, Tioga's strange young man. In it I had used my own experience in trying to compose fire symphonies. Here is the passage to which Milove referred:

"It was several years before we saw Carl again, and again he came to our house.

"Doctor, sir," he said to my father,"Please may I have an opportunity to discuss with you an insight which has come to me? I desperately need to present it to someone with some educational and cultural background. Please, sir?"

Dad was not one to suffer fools gladly but he'd just eaten a fine meal with apple pie. "All right, Carl. Come into the living room and tell me what's on your mind."

I remember some of what Carl said though it didn't make much sense. In essence, he claimed to have discovered a brand new art form, one that combined painting and sculpture and music and much more besides. He told us he'd learned how to build fires so he could predict every color and contour of the flames from one moment to another.

"I arrange my kindling so it will produce a prelude, shaping the main theme of my composition. I've even learned how to create a counterpoint effect. I've composed three flame symphonies already and I can do them every time if I have the same wood..That's the hard part, and also trying to invent a notation that is adequate. I've just started, but look here,

Doctor."

Carl pulled out a large sheet that looked like a musical score except that there were no musical notes on it, just a complicated set of squiggles so far as I could see. He excitedly explained what they meant.

"This one refers to a forked flame, that one to a flame having a single apex; this symbol represents the color and duration of the flame, and that one's for the sound."

He also had symbols for tempo. It was far too complicated for me to follow, even though he quit using those big words as he became more excited.

"And these little dots on the score are sparks, Doctor. By using osage orange or sumac wood I can create a wonderful fanfare of sparks at just the right time. Just think, Doctor, here is the poor man's art form. All he needs is a match...."

Carl suddenly stopped talking and looked my father straight in the eye. "Am I crazy, Doctor?"

My father was polite, but after he ushered Carl out the front door, he made his diagnosis.

"Nutty as a hoot owl," he said."

As the day came to its close I wasn't very happy so I did what I often do to make myself a better mood. I wrote another little U.P. tale, felt good, and went to bed. Here it is:

Drumsticks

People used to say that there were more liars to the square yard in the U.P. than anywhere else in the country. I don't know that this is true but I do know that Tioga, the little forest village where I was born, had the biggest one. His name was Slimber Vester, a saintly looking old scoundrel with a fine white beard, who used to tell his tales in Higley's saloon every Saturday evening when he had a beer or two or three. Here is another of his milder lies.

"I've always liked the drumsticks of a chicken better than any other part," he said, "and I never have yet had my fill of them. Trouble is that a chicken usually has only two legs."

One of the other men at the bar took the bait. "Usually?" he asked. "What you mean, usually. Never was a chicken had any more than two."

"That's what you say. That's what you say, but I know different." Slimber was not offended. He'd had many others who doubted his honesty.

"I learned better one time I guided a feller from Chicago trout fishing on the Paint River near Republic. He was one of these here fly fisherman. Wouldn't use worms and he tells me he wanted not too big a stream nor any with brush on the banks, one with a lot of meadows and a lot of trout. That's asking a lot but I figured the Paint River with its beaver meadows might be what he wanted."

"Yeah," said one of the men at the bar, "but that's a long way from Tioga. How'd you get there?"

"Well, the dude had plenty of money so we rented a horse and buggy from Marchand's Livery Stable. No, not Maude, that pokey old broken down mare. If we'd had her the trip would have taken a whole day. Marchand gave us Celeste who can step along pretty lively if you give her a little taste of the whip "

The men were getting impatient. "But what about those chickens. Slimber? Tell us about them chickens."

"I'm a-coming to it," replied Slimber, lighting his old corncob pipe. "I'm a-coming to it. Anyone feel like buying me another beer?"

Refueled, he continued. "Yep, it's a long way and I could see the man from Chicago was getting restless so I slapped Celeste hard with the reins and she was really galloping when we see a big chicken trotting along beside the buggy and then passing us."

"You're crazy," said a man. "No chicken can run fast as a horse."

"That's what we thought," said Slimber. "The man I was guiding almost lost his eyeballs looking at that chicken".

"Do you see what I see?" he asked me. "That damned chicken has three legs. Do you see three legs?"

"So help me it was true. It had one leg in front and two behind and they were big legs, bigger than you ever seen. And that was why he could run so fast. He'd reach out with the one leg then straddle it with the hind ones and gallop like a bear going up hill. Celeste she was going plenty fast and that chicken passed her like she was standing still."

"That's hard to believe," said Higley, the bartender.

"Yep, I know it is," replied Slimber, "but harder yet is that pretty soon along came three or four more chickens that passed us and all of them had three legs too. I tried to run into one of them, thinking of the fine drumsticks, but it dodged and passed us easily."

"'Well,' the man beside me said, I can't believe it. Whip the horse so I can get a better look.' Just then the road turned and there was a straight stretch ahead so we could see all them three legged chickens up ahead of us and then they turned off up a farmer's lane to the right."

"'Follow them,'" he ordered and soon we came to a farmhouse to see a woman feeding corn to a whole flock of them, all three legged."

"The man steps out and says politely , 'Maam, are these three legged chickens yours? I never see their like before.'

'Guess there aren't any others like them,' she answered. 'We got them from my brother who does research on chicken breeding at the State College and he sent them up here so we could breed them for their drumsticks.'

'Wow!'" said the man. 'One of them drumsticks would be a full meal., Are they too tough?'

'Dunno,' she said. 'We've never been able to catch one."

DAY NINE

My morning greeting to the world had little fervor in it when I poked my head out of the back door. It would be another gray miserable day. Would spring ever come? Knowing I'd have to make sure that depression and negative thoughts would not add to it I made myself some french toast. Alas, it turned out to be soggy and the sugarless maple syrup didn't help any either. What could I do this day to make it enjoyable and significant? I couldn't think of a single thing.

Well then I'd do something that should be done, something I'd put off doing too long. How about putting some new washers in the faucets that had been leaking? No, I was all out of washers and John wouldn't be able to get them until the weekend. Or I could empty the fireplace ashes and put them on the lilacs. Nuts to that. There weren't enough of them. I could dust the upstairs hallway and bedrooms. No, they weren't really dirty.

While I was considering these self suggestions I knew all the time what I should really do: clean and organize my study. Heaven knows it needed it. The project was so unattractive it took an extra cup of coffee and a pipe of Sir Walter Raleigh before I could make myself get out of the comfortable chair. Like Lord Nelson at the naval battle of Trafalgar, I shouted, "England expects every man to do his duty!" OK, study, here I come."

But where to begin? As I looked it over I felt sorry for my children who would have to get rid of the stuff after I died. I knew none of them would live here in the old house; they had their own. They wouldn't want that ancient bronze spear point given me by that stutterer from Iran or the little bust of Nephrite by the one from Egypt nor the stein from Germany nor the wooden fishhook from the Fiji Islands. My son might want to have the ten pound family Bible but would he desire the black jug I found in an abandoned lumber camp? Perhaps Cathy might like to keep the brass spittoon her mother had rescued from my father's hospital and after much polishing had turned it into a lovely vase for our flowers. Would Sue want the glass cage of stuffed birds including the extinct passenger pigeon or should I give it to our museum? And all my treasured books, shell collection and tobacco pipes? Perhaps I should make the bonfire of bonfires out behind the barn? No that would be too hard work and spoil the nest in which I'd laid so many literary eggs.

Under my east bookcase is a space full of boxes of manila

folders which I had put there when I last cleaned my study some years ago. Surely some of those could be discarded. I opened one and found it full of drawings my children had made when they were very young. One was of me, a monkey smoking a pipe. Another folder held all the materials I'd assembled in tracing my family tree back to Jurien Tomasson Van Riper who came to this country from Holland in the sailing ship the Spotted Cow in 1640. I put it in the wastebasket, then took it out again. My son might like to have the information when he too grew old. Let him throw it away if he didn't.

When I opened the third big envelope it was the end of my cleaning spree. In it were notes for more tales about the old U.P., unfinished manuscripts and stories that were completed but had never been published. Though I knew I would never write another Northwoods Reader it was so much fun reading them that I spent the whole day doing so with breaks only for getting the mail and meals and wood for my Happy Hour.

The first tale I read was about an old self taught fiddler named Waino Ohala. a very shy man, whose whole life revolved around his violin. I described how he got his first instrument, how he learned to play it, how it cured his shyness and gave him a lovelife. It told about the barn dances of the time, his battle with the drunk who smashed it. It ended with his final concert out in the woods when unable to play very long because of the arthritic pain that prevented his pressing the strings, he'd shot himself. I'd written it much better than it sounds here. Why hadn't I included it in one of my books? Too tragic? I'd written other sad tales that my readers had loved. Should I dump it in the wastebasket? No, I might want to read it again some day.

The next manuscript I found was a completed story about a morning that my beloved Grampa Gage and I spent collecting holes, mouse holes, fox holes, key holes, holes in the water produced by paddles, caves. It ended with our exploration of the huge one up at the mine that had resulted from a great cave-in that had engulfed two houses and two sleeping men. Throughout the story I had tried to express the fascination that holes hold for men and hounds alike. Grampa had some very funny and enlightening comments. But somehow the tale never really jelled nor could I find a good ending for it.

Next I found a narrative about the trip our family made from Tioga to Iron Mountain in Dad's new 1914 Model-T Ford. Now we can drive it in just an hour but then it took us a whole day each way. The road consisted of just two ruts through a deep hardwood wilderness so thick we often had to use the one man cross cut saw to open the road or to cut some logs to replace those of the corduroy in a swamp. Several times we forded a little stream. I counted forty three deer en route. The story had a lot about that car and its problems and characteristics, the many flat tires that had to be patched on the spot, how it scared the horses of farmers and so on. I never finished that tale because I felt few readers would be interested. I can never bear the thought that some reader might say Ho-Hum.

Another unfinished tale was about how Eino and Emil celebrated a New Year's Day with a two moon toot. (In the U.P. that means you're so intoxicated you see, not one moon, but two.) It was a hilarious tale so far as it went but I couldn't find a good ending that was at all plausible.

One of the best tales was about how Old Man McGee had a fine Christmas after all. I've always enjoyed writing about him and the Easter story I published in one of my Northwoods Readers is a favorite of mine. That's the one about how he celebrated by preaching a sunrise service to the tombstones.

In the folder were a lot of my mulling cards, those on which I'd jotted down items I might use when I did write a new tale. I'll just list the titles because you could make no sense of the stuff I scribbled on them. Here are a few: The Big Fight, The Flu Epidemic, Dad's Toughest Confinement Case, Stealing Apples, Charon Wrestles the Buck, Our Little Orchestra, Sir Launcelot, Our Rooster, The Code, Our Childhood Games, Trapping, The Last Deer Camp, Memorial Day in Tioga. Mullu, Fisheye and the Billygoat, Miss Polson's Battle with Old Blue Balls. And there were a lot more.

Again I wondered where all of them came from. I was a forest spring; the more water that left it, the more came in. Too bad I wouldn't be able to write another book but perhaps I could include one of the tales in this book, a short one. It would have to be an amusing one. I didn't want to end this book tragically. In the folder was a letter from Charlie Shilling that had a good Halloween story. I'd rewrite it for all the readers of my book who have shared bits of their lives with me. Here it is:

A few years back, two of my neighbors, Bill and Emily Smith, were going to a Halloween party at the Legion Hall. Emily is quite a character, always out for a good time. Bill is slow and serious but has a good sense of humor. They decided to dress up in costumes, Bill as the devil and Emily as an angel so she made the costumes for both of them.

The afternoon of the party however Emily came down with one of her bad migraine headaches and when Bill came home she told him she was too sick and that he should go without her. Bill replied that he'd just as soon stay home but Emily told him she'd done a lot of work making that devil costume and wished he'd go without her. She didn't feel like making him any supper and they'd have food at the hall. Bill finally agreed and off he went in the big red suit, horns, tail and all. Emily had done a good job. He really looked like the devil with his mask on.

When he left Emily took a couple of aspirins and lay down to take a nap. After about an hour she woke up feeling fine. After another half hour she was feeling better yet so she decided to go to the party after all. Then she got to thinking that it might be a good time to check up on Bill and to see how he acted around women when she wasn't around. You never knew about these men when they're let loose. When she went to the closet to get her angel costume the thought hit her like lightning that he'd recognize her but if she used the old witch's costume she'd worn many years ago he wouldn't. She found it in the attic along with a pointed hat and ugly mask. Yeah, that would do it. Bill would never know if she disguised her voice.

When she got to the Legion party she saw her big red devil standing at the bar talking sweet stuff with a female, the dirty dog. She went over to them and using a high pitched voice she asked him if he would buy a hot witch a drink too. The devil said sure, she could have anything she wanted.

"What I want, we can't do here," she said, "but buy me a drink and we'll talk about it."

By the time they finished the drink she could have killed that big devil of a husband of hers. He sure was full of the devil inside as well as outside. To test him a bit further, she told him she'd like to know just how long his tail really was and he said, "Fine! Let's go outside and I'll show you under the big pine tree. "

Outside they went but she broke away and fled home. She'd wait up for that two-timing skunk, and see what kind of a lie he would tell. She had him this time and she'd let him have it good. She'd never trust him again. The longer she waited up for Bill to come home, the madder she got. He could fry in hell. She'd make him sweat.

When Bill did come home about one thirty Emily had calmed down some. She would be nice and cool and let him hang himself. "Did you have a nice time at the party?" she asked sweetly. "Did you have any fun?"

"Not really," Bill replied."I had a bite to eat, drank a few beers and sat out in the back room playing cards all evening with Fred and Ed."

"You didn't dance or have fun with some woman?" she inquired.

"No," he answered. "I loaned my costume to Frank and I guess he had a hot time with some old witch."

When I finished typing that tale it was bedtime. I'd been inside almost all that day but it had been another good one.

THE DAY THAT WILL BE OR MIGHT HAVE BEEN

It is mid-winter Down Below. A foot of snow covers my farm and it is very cold. Unlike the dry cold of the U.P. this is piercingly damp and one feels it more intensely or at least in my old age I do. Old bones! Old bones! Damned old bones! Up there in my homeland the sun shines; here it does not. Most of our days are spent beneath gray, cloudy skies. What the hell am I doing down here anyway? Will spring ever come?

I'm not as sure as I once was that I would make it through the winter because lately I've been having a rough time. Twice this month I thought I was going to die, the last episode occurring just two days ago. I won't go into the morbid details but the Old Reaper sure took a good swipe at me with his scythe.

And that is the reason I'm writing about a day that perhaps might be or might have been. I hate to leave this book unfinished and although I had planned to include some other days of my life down here in Portage I'll just pretend that I did survive and tell you what might have occurred when I found myself back in Shangrila.

****

When I awakened John was gone but a fine fire blazed in the fireplace of the big cabin and the smell of coffee made it hard to lie there much longer. On the boards of the bunk above me were the words "Good Morning, Grampa" printed in a childish hand by one of my grandchildren. Ah, it would indeed be a great morning. Despite my bum prognosis I was back in my homeland again, back in my cabin on our lovely wilderness lakes. How the devil had I managed it?

Actually the long trip hadn't been bad at all because in the rented conversion van I had been able to lie down most of the way while John did all the driving except for the long Seney stretch where I took the wheel. Arriving at dusk, I had a snort of scotch while John unpacked and built a fine fire. Then after eating half of one of the pasties we'd picked up en route I hit the sack. Watching the flame shadows flickering on the burnished log walls, I was soon asleep with a smile on my face. It was still there the next morning.

I lay there a bit savoring the moment until the smell of the coffee John had made and the sight of the fire he had started got me out of bed. Opening the door to go to the outhouse in the woods I found myself deeply inhaling that wonderful U.P. air fresh from the waves of Lake Superior. In it were traces of cedar and balsam and the musky smell of deep woods. Fog devils swirled on the lake's surface chasing each other. From beyond Birch Point came the long lorn call of a loon. I almost hugged myself. I was home again!

For just a moment I was tempted to strip off my clothes and plunge nakedly into the lake as so often I'd done as a boy but instead scooped up water in my cupped hands to wash my old face. Cold water! Clean water! Spluttering, I shook the drops off my white beard and let the spring sun tingle it dry before entering the cabin. Lord, I was feeling good.

The years fell from me like those water drops.

Not knowing when John might return for breakfast I poured a cup of coffee to go with some Korpua and a chunk of the smoked whitefish we'd picked up at Naubinway and sat in the big chair before the fire. My wife had bought that chair for me because I'd purchased one for her of the same kind. Hers was sitting by the north window overlooking part of the West Bay and Birch Point. How many hours we'd spent together in those chairs watching the chipmunks and seeing the many changes in the lake's surface. There were times when the lake looked like frosted glass; at others like a dark black mirror. This morning it was very blue with waves bearing white caps surging toward the east and crashing against Herman's Rock where we always put the fish entrails so the bears wouldn't bother us. Herman, our seagull, hadn't found us yet but he will. I chuckled remembering how he had tried to defend that white rock from a tall blue heron last summer. One sharp peck from the heron's bill sent him away squawking. And the time when a bald eagle drove Herman away and ate his food.

To get the smell of the smoked fish off my hands I went to the pump and sink. Ach! The pump had lost its prime as it usually does over the winter when the leathers dry out. Getting a jug of lake water I poured it down the top as I pumped the handle with my other hand, soon felt the pressure building resistance, and out came a rush of water from the spout. It's good water but I hoped John had filled another jug from our big spring on the far bay. I like spring water for my evening whiskey. In deer camp we use the icicles that hang from the roof.

Finally rousing myself I looked out of the other window to see where John might be. Our big cabin sits on a point and from each window you can see a different section of the lake. Perhaps John's boat was in the south bay or the outlet. Looking through the big south window I felt that there was something wrong. Oh yes, we hadn't put up the flag yet on the tall pole by the dock. Milove always hoisted it the moment she arrived. After finding it in the long cupboard bench I soon had the flag waving and saluted both it and her. Cully was back in camp.

The other thing that my wife always did upon arriving was to feed the chipmunks so I took some sunflower seeds to the little tables and ladders that my daughter Sue had constructed when she was in the third grade. Though a little rickety after so many years they were still serviceable. Soon the chipmunk word would get out and we'd have a lot of them scurrying around. The big one, Manchester, (we've had a long series of Manchesters) would be spending so much of his chippie time chasing the others off he'd hardly have time to eat anything himself. I noticed the pancake nail on one of the big cedars where we always hung the extra one or the burned one. I heard a red squirrel unwinding his ratchet and knew he'd be waiting for that first pancake. I remembered the time a huge osprey swooped down on immense but silent wings to snatch a chippie off the feeder. The place was so full of memories they tumbled all over my mind, each one leading to another.

Returning around the corner of the cabin I saw the silly little brass bell and pulled its string. It's tinkle was never loud enough to serve its original purpose which was to call the children to a meal. Instead, it was the Chase -me-Grampa bell. Whenever a grandchild rang it Grampa had to leave whatever he was doing and chase the kid around the cabin. I never failed to respond because I could get my three hugs if I caught him or her. Behind the south east corner of the cabin is a little hummock called Toad Hill on which sits a big chunk of wood. This was their sanctuary because if they could reach it before I caught them they were safe and I got no hugs. Oh, the joyful squealing. Toad Hill was called that because often under the chunk we often found a toad and then had to kiss it.

Just beyond Mr.Toad's hill is our woodshed and wondering about the wood supply I went to it. Rich Waisanen, my caretaker, had filled it with big chunks. John would have to split some for small wood and some cedar for kindling. At the corners of the shed I'd transplanted several sprigs of Virginia Creeper ivy from home some years ago. Had they survived another winter? Yes, there they were. I laid some branches up against the logs so the vines could climb, hoping that eventually they would cover the structure.

The hunger to see the Old Cabin was hard upon me. Would I be able to walk the fourth of a mile to see it? To find out I started up the road, my legs hurting with each step. When I got to the Little Bear's Hole I looked inside the hollow tree to see if there was a message. For years, ever since she was seven, my granddaughter, Jennifer, and I have used it as a postoffice. I pretend to be Little Bear and write notes to her on birch bark and she responds in the same way. Jennifer had been up at the cabin last summer after I had but she was very adult now and I wondered if she had forgotten. Yes, there it was: "Dear Little Bear: I hope you haven't forgotten me for a girl friend in the Porcupineapple Mountains. Please leave me a note. Yours, Jen." Sure made me feel good.

I walked a bit further up the road to where the Upper Lake Trail starts its long way around our lake. Surprisingly it seemed clear and open though I knew that there would be new windfalls along its route for John to cut with the chainsaw. Tempted to follow it to Porcupine Bluff I rested on a log, then decided not to push things. Getting back to the Big Cabin would be all the limping I could handle.

For once I had been wise. Going down the hill was harder than climbing it and I was so exhausted I lay down in the bunk until I heard the outboard motor.

I was down at the dock when John expertly coasted the boat to the sand. A big grin ran around his face as he held up a stringer holding three big bass. "Caught a lot of smaller ones too," he said, "and had a big pike that got tangled in the motor and got away. I always forget to pull it up. I will remember next time. Anyway we've got fish for supper." Stripping off his pants and shoes, he wrestled the old fish cage into the water and dumped the bass into it. Lord, that cage was almost as old as he was. I remember building it after some varmint, probably a mink, had stolen my supper off the fish stringer.

"I'm hungry," John said, looking at his watch. "Hey, it's quarter after eleven. How about pancakes and bacon for an early lunch? Wish we had some cranberries or blueberries to put in the pancakes." I nodded. At home in Portage I rarely have any real appetite but up in the north country I always do. Something about the air, no doubt.

As he mixed the batter and put the bacon in the old cast iron skillet I remembered that once, as a youth, I'd eaten seventeen big pancakes in one sitting. "Make just two for me, Pierre," I said, "and see if you can find the bottle of ersatz maple syrup I brought up. I hate the stuff but it's better than nothing. I'm sure you can find some good maple syrup in the cupboards."

When he opened one of them to look he exclaimed. "Mice! They've sure raised hell over the winter and probably have some young too. I thought I heard some scampering around last night.

Oh what a mess! I'll clean it up this afternoon. Look what they did to the spaghetti!"

"Yeah," I said, "Save some of the bacon grease to mix with the peanut butter for baiting the traps. We'll clean them out of here. I bet they've got a hole in the flashing along the chimney that we'll have to caulk again."

I grinned when he took down the long griddle from the wall and wiped the dust off it. That cast iron has never been washed. It's against the camp law ever since my father brought it to the Old Cabin in 1917 yet it always makes the best pancakes you ever tasted. "Be sure to make enough for the red squirrel and chippies," I said.

John, or Pierre as I call him when he cooks, has come a long way since I first brought him up here five years ago. The pancakes were perfect and I ate three of them. After wiping the dishes I asked John to drive me up to the Old Cabin for my nap. "I may walk back on the trail behind the outhouse," I said, " but if I'm not here by two thirty, come after me."

"I've got to set the minnow traps in the Beaver Dam." he replied. "Why don't you come with me and I'll let you off on the way back? You always liked that spot." When we reached the dam it was obvious that the beavers were still there because the water had backed up almost to the road. I got out of the car to enjoy that beautiful spot again, one that I had seen in my dreams for months. Oh to see it when the fall colors were at their peak. It's breathtaking. As John put some bread in the traps and flung them into the water I felt the new silky green tamarack needles, always a miracle, and soft as a baby's cheek. And there on a sandy spot at the edge of the road I found moose tracks, huge ones, bigger than a cow could make. Perhaps we'll see them again this time, possibly in the marsh near the outlet. I must remember to get out the binoculars. What huge monsters they are, those kings of the wilderness. As we came back from the beaver dam I found myself getting excited. I've felt that way every time since I was a boy, and I could hardly wait to get out of the car at the turnaround. I'm back, Old Cabin. I'm back! That was what Milove always said, and perhaps some of my grandchildren will say it too.

This time I had an added incentive because last summer I saw that its three lower south logs were rotting and I'd asked Rich, my caretaker, to replace them. He and a friend had spent two days doing so and he'd sent me a photo but I wanted to see for myself. A fine job. It would need some additional chinking but now the Old Cabin would last another seventy years for my grandchildren and great grandchildren to enjoy.

As John unlocked the door, I asked him to open the windows and built a little fire in the box stove to get rid of the camp damp that always shows up over winter. After he left, I sat in the big chair for a long time remembering the good times I'd had there as a boy, as a youth, and when I brought Milove there on our honeymoon to find a huge log my friends had wedged in the middle of the upper bunk. I'd made a balsam bed there for us. Now she was gone and I was alone but her ashes had been scattered about the little clearing as mine would also be. She had come back as she had requested, and I too was back with her.

The fire John had built soon warmed the cabin so I got some blankets from the hamper and laid down on them to have my nap. But before I did I found the big nickel watch The Regulars had left when their deer hunting days were over. Once again, after I wound it, the second hand started moving. How often it had ticked on the ledge beside the bunk! Nothing had changed. Not even I. I closed my eyes.

As I lay there a host of memories came back to me, some about The Regulars, Dad's old hunting cronies, when they spent their annual two weeks hunting deer from this old cabin. What fun they had. Big men freed from the responsibilities of work and family, up here they were boys again.

I thought of my own fine summers up here alone learning the ways of the forest creatures, becoming one myself. How I had roamed those deep woods until I knew every foot of them, almost every moss covered rock, the inner sanctuaries of every swamp or clump of huge hemlocks on the hills.

And I thought of Milove and wished she were here beside me. She always wanted to sleep next to the window so she could feel herself a part of the forest and hear the night sounds. I reminded myself that I must tend the little terrace garden I'd made for her near the Big Cabin. Had the arbutus and blue gentians and star flowers she'd transplanted there survived another year? It would need some weeding.

Suddenly I awakened. It was two o'clock on the old watch beside me.

After I went outside I sat for a time on the bench looking at the little clearing where so many good experiences had taken place. Even now I could see remnants of the night fires we'd had when my children were young. How excited they were as night came and the sparks drifted upward. Wide eyed, they would sit there with our arms around them until the night noises made them flee to the safety of the bunks.

And there in the ferns on a warm moonlit night Milove and

I had lain once on the second of August. I know the date because our Susan's birthday is May the second.

I returned to the Big Cabin, not on the road, but on the short cut path that I'd made for my wife so she wouldn't have to walk so far to get to the outhouse. She never could get used to sitting on the log I'd nailed between two trees. "The chipmunks look at me," she protested.

That path is mostly down hill and I had no trouble mainly because I rested often, the first time beside the huge flat topped boulder where I found my son, a little lost boy, trying to climb it. Now he is almost fifty years old but I can still see him after I hoisted him on top of it and called him King of the Woods.

John's Rock

From there the path descends westward. I know every foot of it and could walk it with my eyes shut as I often do in my dreams Down Below. My next resting place was by my Healing Rock, a pyramidal boulder covered with lush moss that for years has given me peace and comfort. I laid my old face against it hoping it would heal me again but when I started walking I knew I had asked too much.

Still descending the hill I found that a big birch tree had fallen across the path. A yellow birch, a tough old giant, it had bested many storms to have grown so tall. As I sat upon its huge trunk I noticed that just beyond it was a row of seven or eight pink lady slippers. That surprised me because they are solitary flowers. Then I saw that they were following a depression filled with rich humus that had once been another fallen tree. And there below me was the shimmering lake....

At this point I will leave this special day unfinished although I know that books should have a tidy ending. Lives are not like that and surprisingly as of this writing my own is unfinished too. As I walk through the shadows of the Valley, may my remaining steps be happy ones. I am determined that they shall be. And may all your steps be happy ones too.

Lady Slipper

EDITOR'S NOTE

Much to my surprise I'm still living and did get back to my U.P. lakes last June for a few days. I'd like to hear from you if you're so inclined.

Cully